"You don't remember me, do you?"

Dylan asked gently.

Her hand shook slightly and she seemed to avoid his gaze on purpose. "Should I?"

"Maybe it wasn't as big a deal for you as it was for me. You were the first girl I ever kissed."

Jennifer retreated to her corner of the sofa. "You're kidding."

"Nope. I was twelve years old and thought you were the prettiest girl I'd ever seen."

"How did you manage to kiss me?"

He leaned back in his chair, enjoying his recollection. "Tommy Bennett bet me a dollar I was too chicken to try."

"You kissed me on a bet?" Laughter tugged at the corners of her luscious mouth, and he experienced an irresistible urge to kiss her again. "I should have pushed you in the lake."

"What made you come back to Memphis?" he asked suddenly.

"I had many happy times here, so naturally I wanted to return."

His policeman's instincts went on alert. But why would anyone lie about something as innocuous as why she chose to live in a certain place?

Unless she had something to hide.

Dear Harlequin Intrigue Reader,

Got a bad case of spring fever? Harlequin Intrigue has the antidote for what ails you. Breathtaking romantic suspense to blast away the cold of winter.

Adrianne Lee brings you the next title in our TOP SECRET BABIES promotion. Tough-guy cop Cade Maconahey could face down any foe, but he was a fish out of water with a baby. Good thing Joanna Edwards showed up when she did to help him out…but what was her real motive? Find out in *Undercover Baby*.

Passion ignites in Debra Webb's next COLBY AGENCY case. Ian Michaels and Nicole Reed go head-to-head in *Protective Custody*—the result is nothing short of explosive. Charlotte Douglas follows up her cross-over Harlequin American Romance-Harlequin Intrigue series, IDENTITY SWAP. Sexy lawman Dylan Blackburn had loved Jennifer Reid from afar, but when he had the chance to love her up close, he'd learned there was a *Stranger in His Arms*.

Finally, Sheryl Lynn winds up her two-book McCLINTOCK COUNTRY miniseries with *Colorado's Finest*. Tate Raleigh combines urban street smarts with a rugged physique and stalwart principles that stand the test of time. He's a devastating opponent to any criminal—and totally irresistible to every woman.

So we hope each one of these fantastic stories jump-starts the season for you. Enjoy!

Sincerely,

Denise O'Sullivan
Associate Senior Editor
Harlequin Intrigue

STRANGER IN HIS ARMS

CHARLOTTE DOUGLAS

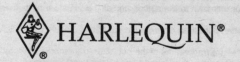

TORONTO • NEW YORK • LONDON
AMSTERDAM • PARIS • SYDNEY • HAMBURG
STOCKHOLM • ATHENS • TOKYO • MILAN • MADRID
PRAGUE • WARSAW • BUDAPEST • AUCKLAND

ISBN 0-373-22611-X

STRANGER IN HIS ARMS

ABOUT THE AUTHOR

Charlotte Douglas has loved a good story since learning to read at the age of three. After years of teaching that love of books to her students, she now enjoys creating stories of her own. Often her books are set in one of her three favorite places: Montana, where she and her husband spent their honeymoon; the mountains of North Carolina, where they're building a summer home; and Florida, near the Gulf of Mexico on Florida's West Coast, where she's lived most of her life.

Books by Charlotte Douglas

HARLEQUIN INTRIGUE
380—DREAM MAKER
434—BEN'S WIFE
482—FIRST-CLASS FATHER
515—A WOMAN OF MYSTERY
536—UNDERCOVER DAD
611—STRANGER IN HIS ARMS*

HARLEQUIN AMERICAN ROMANCE
591—IT'S ABOUT TIME
623—BRINGING UP BABY
868—MONTANA MAIL-ORDER WIFE*

*Identity Swap

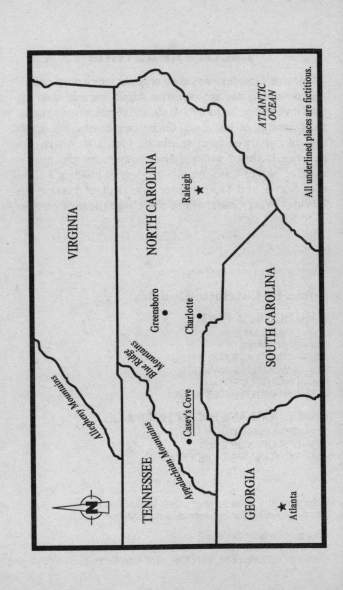

ATLANTIC OCEAN

VIRGINIA

NORTH CAROLINA

Raleigh ★

Greensboro ●

Charlotte ●

Blue Ridge Mountains

SOUTH CAROLINA

Allegheny Mountains

Appalachian Mountains

Casey's Cove ●

TENNESSEE

GEORGIA

Atlanta ★

N

All underlined places are fictitious.

CAST OF CHARACTERS

Dylan Blackburn—A dangerously handsome cop with high principles, a long memory and a love of justice.

Jennifer Reid—A warm and attractive woman with secrets and a killer on her trail.

Miss Bessie Shuford—Matriarch of Casey's Cove and Jennifer's employer.

Jarrett Blackburn—Dylan's older brother who raises Christmas trees.

Johnny Whitaker—Dylan's best friend and fellow cop who died tragically.

Raylene—Café owner, town gossip and Jennifer's best friend.

Sissy McGinnis—A lonely little girl Jennifer takes under her wing.

Larry Crutchfield—An Atlanta attorney with a dubious past.

Michael Johnson—A hired killer who'll do whatever it takes to fulfill his contract.

Prologue

Slinging her hastily filled backpack over her shoulder, she raced toward the front door, but skidded to a stop before she reached it. A huge figure on the porch was silhouetted against the etched glass.

He had come for her.

Pivoting on her heel, she sprinted to the rear of the house, eased out the back door noiselessly and ran across the yard. Just as she was clambering up the fence to gain access to the alley, the neighbor's dog howled.

Running footsteps thundered behind her, and as she hoisted herself over the fence top, a hand snagged her ankle. With a fierce kick that contacted with flesh and bone, eliciting a curse from her pursuer, she freed herself and dropped into the alleyway.

Without a backward look, she kicked up dust racing toward the main street, clogged with going-to-work traffic. As she reached the curb, a bus approached.

There is a God, she thought and breathed a prayer of thanks.

The bus slowed and stopped, and she hopped on.

The doors closed behind her, and the bus picked up speed.

Only then did she dare risk a look behind.

He stood on the curb for an instant, glowering with rage. Then he turned and sprinted toward his car, parked in front of her house. Her only hope was to exit the bus without him catching her.

And if she could pull that off, she needed to disappear.

Permanently.

Chapter One

Four months later

Grinning like a man who'd won the lottery, Officer Dylan Blackburn eased his patrol car down the steep drive from Miss Bessie Shuford's mountaintop home.

His luck that morning had been twofold. First, on his visit with Miss Bessie, the matriarch of Casey's Cove, he had escaped without having to consume one of her infamous cinnamon buns. Not that he didn't love good food, but Miss Bessie's favorite creations had all the grace and flavor of a shot put and sat just about as heavy on the stomach. If he hadn't been unwilling to offend the sweet old woman, he'd have shellacked one for use as a doorstop at the station years ago.

The second source of his good humor was the latest news Miss Bessie had shared. The ninety-five-year-old spinster had just hired a new assistant, a former summer visitor to Casey's Cove whom Dylan remembered well. The newcomer was setting up housekeeping in Miss Bessie's guest house, located a few hundred yards down the mountain from the Shuford mansion, and he was on his way to renew an old acquaintance.

Dylan parked his cruiser in the guest-house drive, checked in with the station's dispatcher and climbed out of the car. Miss Bessie's property, which included the entire mountainside, had the best view of the valley, and he paused to take in the glorious fall day with its cloudless blue sky reflected on Lake Casey, spread out below the autumn-leaved mountains. The tiny town of Casey's Cove edged its western shore.

The mountain air was cool and exhilarating with a hint of the pungent tang of woodsmoke. He inhaled deeply, thinking, as he did several times a day, that he lived and worked in the finest place in the world. Casey's Cove was a great place to be a cop. Especially if you hated crime. The serene little hamlet deep in the Smoky Mountains of North Carolina had the lowest crime rate in the state.

With one fatal exception.

Reluctant to spoil a perfect day, he pushed the bloody memory from his mind, but he knew it would return. It always did. Especially in his unwanted dreams.

He turned his attention to the guest house, a miniature version of Miss Bessie's grandiose Victorian mansion, nestled beneath two ancient hickories shimmering in golden autumnal splendor. The wide, welcoming front porch with gingerbread fretwork was surrounded by foundation plantings of burning bush, glowing with all the colors of their fiery namesake. With eager anticipation, Dylan climbed the stairs and knocked on the screen door.

Nobody answered.

The front door with its stained-glass panels stood open, and he could see into the sunny front room. With her back to him, a young woman knelt on her hands and knees before the sofa, pushing the attachment of a vintage Hoover beneath the furniture with all the determination of a crusader battling evil.

Dylan knocked again and shouted his presence, but the high-pitched roar of the outmoded vacuum cleaner drowned all other sounds.

He watched for a moment, intrigued by the sight of the small, rounded derriere, nicely shaped and smoothly covered by tightly-stretched denim, bobbing in mesmerizing rhythm with the woman's sweeping movements as she cleaned.

Then, feeling shamefully like a voyeur, he remembered his business, dragged his gaze from the enticing spectacle, and stepped inside.

"Hello," he bellowed, but he couldn't raise his voice above the noise. The woman remained unaware of his presence. Resigned, he strode across the room and tapped her on the shoulder.

With a piercing shriek that overpowered the Hoover's mechanical growl, she leapt upright and straightened in panic. He reacted quickly, but not fast enough. The crown of her head slammed into his nose. The room dimmed, and he stumbled backwards.

"Careful!" he heard her warn after shutting off

the raucous vacuum, her voice honeyed and soft, even when startled.

His vision still clouded, he felt her grab him by the biceps and guide him toward a chair. Sinking gratefully into its depths, he shook his head, attempting to restore his sight and quell his dizziness.

"Stop," she commanded sharply. "Sit still!"

Too dazed to argue, he complied. Her footsteps retreated. By the time she returned, his vertigo remained, but his sight was restored.

He focused on the woman in front of him, and her enchanting appearance hit him like a kick to the gut. The pretty twelve-year-old of that long ago summer had grown up. And how. Slender with curves in all the right places, she had the greenest eyes he'd ever seen, the color of spring leaves on the mountainside. They matched the green of the long-sleeved shirt she wore, untucked and knotted at her narrow waist, its snug fit accentuating small, firm breasts. Her golden hair was pulled back and tied by a scarf, but rebellious curls fell over her forehead and around her ears. Her pixie-shaped face would have been beautiful under different circumstances, but it now wore a look of absolute horror.

"You're bleeding all over yourself and my living room." She thrust a cold damp towel into his hands.

A downward glance revealed she was right. Her head-butt to his nose had created a gusher that had spattered his white uniform shirt with blood.

"Sorry," he mumbled into the towel he pressed to his nose.

"A bloody nose is no more than you deserve."

She sounded winded as well as angry, as if she hadn't recovered from the fright he'd given her. "Even if you are a cop, you have no right barging in and scaring a body to death in her own home."

"I knocked. Several times."

As if unsatisfied with the job he was doing, she took the towel from him and dabbed at his nose. Even over the coppery smell of blood, he could detect the delectable scent of honeysuckle and sunshine. She smelled as good as she looked.

She stopped wiping his face and stepped back, evidently confident his bleeding had ceased. "Take off your shirt," she ordered.

"What?"

"Bloodstains. If I don't rinse them in cold water now, they'll never come out."

His uniforms weren't cheap, so he didn't have to be persuaded to do as she asked. With a few swift movements, he unbuttoned his shirt, shucked it off and handed it to her.

"T-shirt, too."

He yanked the bloodstained garment over his head and tossed it to her.

"I'll be right back," she said in her take-charge fashion. "Light the fire, so you don't get cold. Or I can bring you a blanket."

"No, thanks. I'm fine."

After his unusual confrontation with the most attractive and unnerving female he'd ever met, *cold* was the last thing he felt. However, he obligingly knelt by the fireplace and touched a match to the ready-laid logs and kindling. He could hear water running in the adjacent kitchen and the clink of dishes.

He returned to his chair, and she re-entered the room with a tray. "Thought you might like some coffee to warm you up. It's a fresh pot."

He took the mug she offered and declined a cookie from the plate she passed.

"They're ambrosia cookies. Made them myself. Unless you'd prefer some of Miss Bessie's cinnamon buns—" Her amazing green eyes twinkled with mischief.

"Cookies are fine, but I'm really not hungry," he said hastily.

She smiled, an expression of such unparalleled beauty it almost took his breath away. "I see you're acquainted with Miss Bessie's specialty."

He returned her grin. "I keep a large bottle of Maalox in my patrol car for my visits to her house. Only time I ever had a worse bellyache was from eating too many green apples when I was a kid."

She took her own mug and curled long, slender legs into the corner of the sofa nearest him, graceful as a feline. "Is this an official visit, Officer—?"

"Blackburn." He silently cursed his own thickheadedness. What kind of cop was he that the sight of a pretty woman could make him forget his duty? "Dylan Blackburn."

He watched for a sign of recognition at the mention of his name, but none registered on her pretty face. Evidently he hadn't made the impression on her that she had on him that summer long ago.

"And you're Jennifer Thacker."

As if he'd startled her again, her head snapped up in alarm, and he was glad this time his battered nose was well out of range.

"Jennifer Reid. Thacker's my maiden name. How do you know that?"

"Miss Bessie gave me a copy of your employment application."

"Why?" Her eyes had taken on a hunted look, like those of a wild nocturnal animal caught in a sudden light.

"Just routine. As Miss Bessie's assistant, you'll be helping out occasionally at the day-care center she sponsors. Our department runs background checks on everyone who works with children in this town. Just a precaution."

"What kind of background check? I already gave Miss Bessie references."

"We run a search of state and national computers to see if you've ever served time or have an outstanding warrant."

She relaxed at his explanation, but not much, and he wondered if she had something to hide.

"The stains should be out by now." She jumped to her feet and rushed back to the kitchen as if happy to end the conversation. Again he heard water running, the slam of a door and the sound of a clothes dryer. She returned with the coffeepot and topped up his mug.

Gazing at her up close, he had a hard time reconciling the vivacious woman before him with the image of his summer sweetheart from the year he turned twelve. Young Jennifer Thacker had been cool and distant. In retrospect, he suspected her attitude had been the result of extreme shyness. But there was nothing shy about Jennifer Reid, the widow Miss Bessie had recently hired.

"You don't remember me, do you?" he asked.

Her hand shook slightly as she filled her own mug, and she seemed to avoid his gaze on purpose. "Should I?"

"Maybe it wasn't as big a deal for you as it was for me."

"It?"

"You were the first girl I ever kissed."

She retreated to her corner of the sofa. "You're kidding."

"Nope. I was twelve years old and thought you were the prettiest girl I'd ever seen. Especially since you wouldn't have anything to do with us locals."

"Aunt Emily was very strict. I wasn't allowed much latitude. How did you manage to kiss me?"

For a fleeting second, he wondered why she hadn't remembered. Her forgetting what, to him, had been a momentous event, tweaked his ego. He leaned back in the chair, enjoying his recollection. With logs popping and hissing in the fireplace, the aroma of coffee filling the air, the spectacular fall colors visible through the bay window, he couldn't remember a more perfect day—except the one that long-ago summer when he'd kissed little Jenny Thacker.

"You used to sunbathe on the dock of the place where you stayed down by the lake," he said. "Like clockwork. I knew exactly when you'd be there."

''And you just ran up and kissed me?'' She raised her feathery eyebrows.

He couldn't judge whether her expression was astonishment or amusement, but the delectable curve of her lip made him long to kiss her again. A kiss she would remember this time. Realizing he was still on duty, he squashed the urge. ''I was only a kid, remember? And besides, Tommy Bennett bet me a dollar I was too chicken to try.''

''You kissed me on a bet?'' Laughter tugged at the corners of her luscious mouth, and again he experienced the irrepressible desire to kiss her. ''I should have pushed you in the lake.''

''You just sat there, stunned. Didn't say a word.''

''And you?''

''I took off. But I bought you candy with my winnings. Left it on your doorstep the next day. Then I learned you'd gone home to Memphis that morning. You never came back to Casey Cove. Until now.''

She shook her head sadly. ''Aunt Emily— my great-aunt actually couldn't stand the trip from Memphis after that. Her arthritis crippled her toward the end.''

''Why did you come back now?''

''This was her favorite spot.''

''Whose?''

Jennifer seemed flustered, and what looked like fear flickered briefly in her eyes. ''Aunt Emily's, of course. We had many happy times here, so naturally I wanted to return.''

His policeman's instincts went on alert. Something about her answer rang off-key, but he couldn't put his finger on it. Besides, why would anyone lie about something as innocuous as why she chose to live in a certain place?

Unless she had something to hide.

Dylan pushed the suspicion from his mind. Maybe the blow to his nose had scrambled his brains. He sensed nothing sinister about the delectable Jennifer Reid. Quite the contrary.

"I have a few more questions," he said, "then I can let you get back to your cleaning."

She scrunched her face in a charming grimace. "It's a nasty job, but somebody has to do it."

"The inquiry or the cleaning?"

"Both." She laughed with a rich throaty sound and seemed to truly relax for the first time since his arrival. "Fire away, Officer Blackburn."

Dylan had left her employment form on the clipboard in his car, but he recalled all the pertinent details.

"You stated that you're a widow?"

She nodded. "My husband died almost a year ago."

She exhibited a significant lack of grief. Maybe her marriage hadn't been a happy one. "Is that when you left Memphis?"

"There were too many details to take care of right after he died. But by June I had settled his estate, and I wanted to get away to escape the memories."

He wondered briefly whether those memories had been good ones and why she had omitted saying so. "You mentioned references earlier. Why no references from Memphis?"

The glimmer of alarm returned to her eyes, and she clinched her well-manicured hands tightly in her lap. "I have no living relatives. And I was never employed until after I left Memphis. If you have Miss Bessie's form, you have the name of my employer in Nashville."

"Why Nashville?" His question was more personal curiosity than official. The grown-up Jennifer interested him even more than she had as a pre-teen.

She shrugged. "It was close. And I love people and country music, so it seemed like a good choice."

"You worked as a waitress at the Grand Ole Opry resort?"

"I married right out of high school and never learned a profession or trade."

"How did you come to work for Miss Bessie?" He hated having to interrogate her, but it was part of his job. So far, Casey's Cove had been spared the sexual predators and assorted deviants who had preyed on children of other communities. It was his responsibility to keep the youngsters of his small town safe, even if it meant asking apparently meaningless or even embarrassing questions of newcomers.

The frightened look had disappeared from her eyes. Jennifer unclenched her hands, leaned forward, and helped herself to a cookie from the plate on the tray. "I saw her ad for an assistant in the Asheville paper."

"Asheville? You mean Nashville?"

She had taken a bite of the cookie, but it must have gone down wrong, because she choked and coughed before answering. "Asheville. I'd come to North Carolina to see the mountains in their fall colors. I had planned to visit Casey's Cove anyway, so Miss Bessie's ad seemed like an answer to a prayer."

Her attitude was too off-handed. The woman was hiding something, but he didn't have a clue what it might be. He had to be certain she wasn't a threat to Miss Bessie or the children at the day-care center.

"Isn't there someone in Memphis I can contact for a reference?" he said.

She shifted uneasily, a movement not lost on his trained eye. "My former in-laws, but I left them off my reference list on purpose."

"Why?"

"They never liked me. I hate to think what kind of recommendation they'd give me."

Another indication of a less-than-perfect marriage. But lots of folks had unhappy unions. That didn't make them unfit for employment. He wished he wasn't getting mixed signals from his intuition. He liked the woman, and Miss Bessie with her amazing ability to instantly gauge a person's character had hired her on the spot.

But he'd bet his pension Jennifer Reid was hiding something, something that caused her remarkable green eyes to darken with fear when certain aspects of her past were mentioned.

Stymied by his inability to put his finger on what had frightened her, he knew the interview was over. Jennifer wasn't going to divulge information she didn't want to, especially to a lawman sitting shirtless in her living room, whom she'd only just met.

"That's all I need for now," he said.

"For now? What else is there?" Her face flushed with dismay.

"Just the computer background checks, like I said before." He noted the visible easing of tension in her muscles. "Now, if I can have my shirt, I'll get out of your way."

"If you'll wait a few minutes, I'll iron it for you."

He shook his head. "I have a fresh one in my locker at the station. I'll change when I get there."

She retrieved his shirts from the kitchen and stood quietly while he donned them, still warm from the dryer. He headed for the door, then stopped. "Hope you'll enjoy your time in Casey's Cove, Ms. Reid."

She had followed him to the door and held out one slender, well-shaped hand. "Thank you."

He clasped her small hand in his own large one, enjoying the warm, soft sensation of her skin against his.

"And I'm sorry about your nose," she added with obvious sincerity.

He dropped her hand and rubbed his aching nose ruefully. "Guess that comes with the territory."

"Territory?" She cocked her head to one side in puzzlement, an appealing gesture that made him reluctant to leave.

"That's what I get," he said with a laugh, "for sticking my nose in other people's business—even if it is my job."

She smiled again, and before he changed his mind and lingered, he hurried out the door to his patrol car.

AT THE SOUND of the police car disappearing down the drive, Jennifer collapsed in the chair where Officer Dylan Blackburn had been sitting. She hadn't counted on a run-in with the law, not on her first day in town.

She tried without success to will her knees to stop shaking. He'd scared her senseless, touching her shoulder when she'd thought she was alone in the house. It was a wonder her panicked scream hadn't carried all the way up the mountain to Miss Bessie's place.

And the sight of him had unnerved her as much as his touch. First, his uniform. Since last June, her defenses went on instant alert at the presence of any law-enforcement officer. Some might call it guilty conscience.

She called it self-preservation.

After the uniform, she had focused on the man. How could she not, when he'd been so big, six-foot-two at least, and muscled in a whipcord-lean way that left no question of his strength? Those deep brown eyes, like heat-seeking missiles, seemed to miss nothing, and she'd felt he could read every secret ever written on her soul, just by looking at her. The feeling wasn't pleasant, not with the secrets she had to keep.

His face was too rugged to call handsome, but the strong lines of his forehead and jaw, the straight perfection of his nose—well, perfect before she'd bashed it with her head—combined to make him as appealing a man as she'd ever met.

And when he'd stripped to the skin, she'd been

glad the bloodstained shirts had given her an excuse to leave the room or she might have stood gawking like an idiot in admiration of his powerful biceps and the well-formed muscles of his deeply tanned chest.

Yes, indeed, Officer Dylan Blackburn was one amazingly attractive man, and he had laughing eyes and a sense of humor to boot.

She sprang to her feet. What the devil was she thinking? The last thing she needed was involvement with a policeman, for Pete's sake. She grabbed the Hoover attachment from where she'd dropped it earlier and was about to restart the cacophonous machine when a car pulled into her driveway.

Her heart thudded with alarm. Had Officer Blackburn returned with more probing questions?

"Yoo-hoo, Jennifer?" Miss Bessie's soft, drawling voice floated up from the bottom of the front steps.

With a sigh of relief, Jennifer stepped onto the porch to greet her new employer. "Hi, Miss Bessie."

"Mind if I come up?"

Jennifer descended the steps and assisted the older woman up the steep stairs. For a woman in her mid-nineties, Miss Bessie was extremely agile. She plopped into a wicker chair on the porch, placed her feet, shod in neon-laced sneakers, onto a footstool, and waved Jennifer into a chair opposite.

"It's warming up." The little woman, with bones fragile as a bird's, fanned herself with a lace-trimmed handkerchief. "Indian summer."

"Would you like something cool to drink?"

"No, child, I just came by to chat. Figured since

you're going to be in Casey's Cove for a while, you ought to know something about the place.'' Bessie studied her with bright blue eyes. "How much do you remember?''

Jennifer shook her head. She wished people would stop asking her questions she couldn't answer. "Not much. My visits here were a long time ago.''

The old woman settled back in her chair, and the wicker creaked beneath her slight weight. She pointed to the panorama that stretched below them like a topographical map. "See how the town hugs the west shore of the lake?''

Jennifer nodded.

"When my daddy came to Casey's Cove over a hundred years ago as the town's first doctor, that area was several hundred feet up the mountain from Casey's Creek.''

"Where was the lake?''

"Didn't exist. Not until several decades later when one of FDR's work projects dammed the creek and created Lake Casey. Underneath all that water,'' Bessie waved her arm to take in the thousands of acres the immense lake covered, "are the ruins of several farms, homesteads, even a church, all condemned when the creek was dammed for the hydroelectric plant at the eastern end of the lake.''

Jennifer shivered at the thought of the ancient buildings rotting beneath the lake's surface. Her peaceful retreat had suddenly acquired a sinister aura.

"What happened to all the folks who lived there?'' she asked.

"They moved out of the valley or farther up the

mountains," Miss Bessie said. "Casey's Cove hasn't changed since then. The population remains pretty much the same. Sparse in winter and spring with just us locals. A few hundred extra summer and fall residents. Halfbacks, we call 'em—"

"Football players?"

Miss Bessie giggled like a young girl. "Yankees. Folks who moved down to Florida from the North then came halfway back, as far as North Carolina. And we also get the occasional passing-through tourists."

"If there're only a few hundred year-round residents, how many children are in your day-care center?" Jennifer asked.

"About twenty."

"That's a lot for such a small town."

"Times are hard," Bessie said, "and the women in Casey's Cove have to work. Some clean and cook at the inns and hotels around the lake. Others commute to Sylva to work in the shops in town or at the university." She stared over the lake without looking at Jennifer. "I have a special assignment for you at the center."

"Bookkeeping?" Jennifer said, remembering her employment interview.

"There's that, of course," Bessie said. "But there's more. There's a little girl who needs you."

"I don't have any experience with children," Jennifer admitted. "I told you that in my interview."

"You have a kind heart," Bessie said. "That's all you'll need. And you'll fall in love with Sissy McGinnis the minute you lay eyes on her."

"Sissy—?"

"She's four years old. Her mother is in the hospital, undergoing chemotherapy for cancer. Sissy's living with her aunt while her mother's away. I figured since you were orphaned young and raised by your aunt, you'd have something in common with the girl."

"What about her father?" Jennifer said.

Miss Bessie grimaced. "Low-down worthless skunk took off as soon as he learned Sissy was on the way. Nobody's seen him since."

At a loss as to how she could help the girl, Jennifer asked, "What do you want me to do?"

"Her aunt works days and is bone-tired at night. Sissy needs a grown-up who can help her through this trying time. I figure you'll do just fine."

"You're giving me more credit than I deserve," Jennifer protested. "I don't even know how to start."

"When you go to work on the books tomorrow," Bessie said, "have Sissy help you."

"But you said she's only four."

"You'll think of something," Miss Bessie said breezily and pushed to her feet. "Now, drive me back to the house. You can keep the car for running errands and driving back and forth to the day-care center."

Jennifer went inside and grabbed her purse. As she stepped back onto the porch and was closing the front door, her gaze fell on the empty mug beside the large chair in the living room, reminding her of Dylan Blackburn's visit. With the policeman's prying questions and the responsibility of a four-year-old, Jennifer's arrival in Casey's Cove had quickly gone from serene to unsettled.

DYLAN ENTERED the tiny brick building that served as Casey's Cove's police station and jail. At the front desk Sandy Griffin, the dispatcher, lifted her eyebrows at the sight of his wrinkled shirt. Her fingers flew over a skein of yarn and a crochet needle as she worked a new afghan between radio calls.

The plump, middle-aged woman appraised him with gray eyes that matched her hair. "How's your stomach?"

"Fine," he said with a grin. "Miss Bessie was so excited about her new assistant she forgot to offer cinnamon buns."

"Lucky you. Did you meet the new arrival?"

"Yeah."

Sandy dropped her crochet needle and yarn to her lap. "Is that all you're going to tell me?"

"What else is there?" Dylan answered evasively. He took a seat at his desk and called up a screen on his computer.

"What does she look like, for starters?" Sandy, like every other resident of Casey's Cove, had an insatiable curiosity where outsiders were concerned.

"Pretty," Dylan answered.

"And?" Sandy prodded. "What aren't you telling me, Dylan Blackburn?"

"I don't know." He scratched his head in confusion. "Something about her isn't right."

Sandy's eyes widened. "Miss Bessie didn't hire a crazy woman?"

Dylan smiled and shook his head. "Her mental state is fine, for all I can tell. But I get the strangest feeling she's hiding something."

"You ought to know. You've got the best nose for trouble in town."

"In all those be-on-the-lookout flyers you process every day," Dylan said, "have you ever seen a reference to a Jennifer Reid?"

"Jennifer Reid." Sandy scrunched her plump face in concentration and accessed her phenomenal memory. "I've seen that name before."

Dylan's heart sank. He had hoped his hunch was wrong, that Jennifer Reid wasn't in some kind of trouble.

"It was last June," Sandy said. "A missing person's report. Came with a picture and complete description."

"Is it in the file?"

The dispatcher shook her head. "A couple weeks later a bulletin came through that the woman had been found, so I tossed both papers."

The missing person's report didn't correspond with Jennifer Reid's story—not unless she'd left Memphis for Nashville without telling anyone. But why would she have done that?

Sandy's memory of every paper that came across her desk was exceptional, so he pressed for more information, dreading what he might hear. "Did the missing person's report hint that Jennifer was in any kind of trouble?"

Sandy shook her head and picked up her crocheting again. "Was she wanted for a crime, you mean?

No, it was a straightforward missing person's report. She had disappeared from home. You met the woman. You think she's trouble?''

Dylan remembered the pixie face, dancing green eyes, and take-charge attitude. "I hope not. But there's only one sure way to find out.''

He turned to his computer keyboard, checked his clipboard, and typed Jennifer Reid's name, description, Social Security and driver's license numbers into the national crime computer search engine. The inner workings of the machine clicked and whirred.

He leaned back in his chair and waited. If she was wanted by the authorities, he'd know soon enough.

Chapter Two

Jennifer parked Miss Bessie's new Mercedes at the end of Main Street, climbed out, and surveyed the tiny lakeside community. She had been in Casey's Cove only a week, but already it felt like home.

Better yet, it felt *safe*.

The town was practically deserted this Saturday morning with just a few residents and even fewer tourists on the street. Jennifer wasn't surprised, however, because Miss Bessie had explained the lull between the end of the heavy summer tourist trade and the beginning of crowds of leaf-watchers when the mountain leaves reached their prime fall color.

Content with the freedom of her first day off, she strolled past the farmers' market with its stacks of bright pumpkins, baskets of ripe apples, shocks of Indian corn, and pots of brilliant chrysanthemums. Next door, in Ben Morgan's real-estate office, color snapshots of seasonal rentals lined the picture window.

Across the street, the wide doors of the Artisans' Hall were flung open, and Jennifer could see the potters working inside, wet clay up to their elbows as they threw ceramic mugs and vases on their wheels. In another section of the open building, people were fashioning baskets from wild vines and furniture from willow twigs and branches.

Next to the Artisans' Hall stood the police station, and she wondered if Dylan Blackburn was working the weekend shift. She hadn't seen or heard from him since his initial visit, which she supposed was good news. If his crime computers had spat out any surprises, surely he would have told her by now.

She paused for a last look at the marina on the lake's edge, where pontoons and paddle boats were moored for renting by sightseers. The morning mist steamed off the cold water, and the rising sun backlit the peaks of the surrounding mountains like a Thomas Kincaid painting. Despite her initial scare by Dylan Blackburn, she had decided Casey's Cove was the perfect place to hide.

With a light heart, she stepped inside Raylene's Lakeside Café to the accompaniment of a tiny bell over the door. Ben Morgan sat at the counter, chatting with Grover, the short-order cook, and a couple of farmers from the market occupied a corner table.

Jennifer returned Grover's wave and slipped into a window booth with a view of the lake.

"Morning, Jennifer. What can I getcha?"

Raylene, the café's owner and waitress appeared at Jennifer's elbow. A pretty woman whose face was beginning to show its age and who walked as if her feet hurt constantly, Raylene had befriended Jennifer during her first visit a week ago. Since then, Jennifer had eaten at least one meal a day at the café, partly because of the company, but also because of the food. She didn't know if the mountain air made everything taste better or if Grover had the talent of a gourmet chef, but she looked forward to her daily visit's to Raylene's.

With her appetite piqued by her early-morning stroll, Jennifer requested a western omelet and grits and sipped coffee while Grover filled her order. In a few minutes, the waitress returned with a plate overflowing with food.

"I should have asked for half portions." In spite of her hunger, Jennifer observed the liberal serving with skepticism. "I'll never eat all that."

Raylene grinned and patted her teased hair. "Grover's decided he likes you. He always pads the plates of his favorite customers."

Jennifer knew the routine. She took a bite of the steaming omelet and nodded her approval to Grover, who waited anxiously behind the counter. "It's delicious."

Satisfied with Jennifer's praise, Grover turned back to his conversation with Ben Morgan.

Raylene poured an extra cup of coffee from the serving table and returned to the booth. Her worried expression etched fresh, fine lines around her eyes. "Can I talk to you a minute?"

Jennifer tensed at the seriousness in the older woman's voice. "Please, sit."

The waitress had already proved an invaluable source of information about the town. Not much happened that Raylene didn't either witness or overhear in the café, and she seemed happy to fill Jennifer in on all the latest gossip. But the waitress's tone this morning was somber, not gossipy.

"So—" Jennifer hoped the solemnity of Raylene's news had nothing to do with her. "What's up?"

Raylene took a long sip of her coffee, set down her cup, and gave Jennifer a searching look. "Do you have a sister?"

Jennifer shook her head. "I'm an only child. Why?"

"There was a man in here yesterday. With a picture."

Sudden panic gripped her. Sweat slicked her palms, and her heart pounded so fiercely, the blood rushing in her ears momentarily blocked all other sounds.

Dear God, had he found her?

She took a drink of coffee while she pulled herself together. "What kind of picture?"

"One of them studio portrait types." Raylene assumed a pose. "You know, a glamour shot. I always meant to have mine done over in Asheville, but shoot, now I'm too damn old."

Jennifer gripped her coffee mug and tried to hang on to her shattered nerves. "Whose picture was it?"

Raylene shrugged. "He said a name, but I didn't recognize it. He wanted to know if I'd ever seen the woman."

Jennifer was having trouble breathing. "Had you?"

The waitress shook her head. "Nope. But she sure

did favor you. 'Cept her hair was long, straight and red and she had a ton more freckles than you do.''

Jennifer forced herself to ask the next question. ''What did you tell him?''

''Said I'd never seen the woman.''

Jennifer attempted to hide her relief. ''Why was he looking for her?''

''Said she was some long-lost relative his ailing grandmother wanted to see before she died—but he was lying through his teeth.''

''How could you tell?''

''Honey, I've spent my whole life around men. I can spot a liar a mile off.'' Raylene swirled coffee in her cup. ''He was hard-looking, big and tough, with a face that never smiled. Looked like he'd as soon spit on you as speak. That kinda man don't do no favor for his old grandma.''

''Did he show anyone else the picture?''

Raylene shook her head. ''I told him I saw everyone who came and went in Casey's Cove. If I hadn't seen her, nobody had. He just climbed in his big ol' black SUV and hauled buggy.''

Jennifer couldn't swallow. Grover's tasty omelet had turned to ashes in her mouth. She pushed her plate away.

''That wasn't you, was it?'' Raylene eyed the barely touched food, then focused on Jennifer, her heavily mascaraed eyes filled with concern. ''You're not in some kind of trouble, are you, hon?''

Jennifer pulled the plate back, picked up her fork, and compelled herself to smile. ''Not me. You can ask Officer Dylan Blackburn. He ran all kinds of background checks on me when Miss Bessie hired me.''

Raylene leaned back in the booth with a sigh of relief, apparently satisfied with the explanation. She grinned. ''So you've met our Dylan?''

Jennifer breathed easier with the change of subject. ''The day I arrived.''

Raylene pursed her lips and shook her head. ''He's a heartbreaker, that one. He's got every unmarried woman in the cove making cow-eyes over him.''

''I'm surprised a man that good-looking isn't already taken,'' Jennifer said.

''Dylan's a real straight arrow,'' Raylene said in the conspiratorial voice she used when imparting her juiciest gossip. ''Has zero tolerance for liars, cheats and lawbreakers.''

Jennifer winced inwardly. Raylene's comment hit home. ''That must make him a good cop.''

''Casey's Cove is lucky to have him, but his strong moral principles make him tough to live up to. A woman would have to be a saint to meet Dylan's criteria, and we've got more sinners than saints in this valley.''

''You make him sound harsh.'' Jennifer remembered his attention to duty and detail when he interviewed her the previous week, but he'd seemed friendly enough.

Raylene shook her head. ''Not harsh. Dylan has a deep love for the people he protects, and as for his strict code, he's toughest on himself. When he finally finds the right woman, she's going to be a very lucky girl.''

Jennifer had been impressed with the officer, had admired his good looks and friendly nature. She was grateful for the information from Raylene—but she'd keep her distance from the appealing officer with the strict moral values.

Even if she was interested in Dylan Blackburn, *she* was no saint. Not by a long shot. The lies she'd told would fill a bushel basket. Not to mention the laws she'd broken.

"For the last two years," Raylene continued, "Grover's been running a pool, and the locals are placing their bets on who'll be the lucky woman to haul Dylan to the altar."

Jennifer dragged her attention from her guilty thoughts to Raylene's comments. "Any odds-on favorites?"

"Nope." Raylene pushed to her feet as the bell jingled over the door signaling another customer. She leaned toward Jennifer and winked. "The field's wide-open if you're interested. I can have Grover add your name to the pool."

Before Jennifer could decline, Raylene turned her attention to her newcomer. Jennifer gripped her coffee mug to keep her hands from trembling. The discussion of Dylan, interesting as it was, hadn't made her forget that a menacing stranger had recently appeared in the small hamlet of Casey's Cove searching for a woman who looked like her.

Coincidence?

She didn't think so. But how on earth had he managed to find her in this backwoods? And, even more important, was he still out there, looking for her? Or had Raylene convinced him the woman he searched for wasn't in the area?

She was so lost in thought, she didn't hear the jingling bell announce another arrival, didn't notice his approach until his tall, vast shadow fell across the table of the booth where she sat.

"Mind if I join you?"

She jumped at the question, sloshing coffee from her tightly clenched mug onto the tabletop. Fearing the worst and tensing her muscles to flee, she glanced up.

Dylan Blackburn stared down at her, looking more incredibly handsome and alarmingly dangerous than he had on his first visit several days ago.

A sigh of relief that he wasn't Raylene's menacing stranger whooshed involuntarily from her lungs, while her heart raced with residual fear. Afraid to speak lest fright show in her voice, she nodded and waved him to the seat Raylene had vacated.

He was staring at her too intently with that eagle-sharp gaze of his, and she wondered how many law-breakers had cracked and confessed under that look.

"Sorry if I startled you," he said.

"My fault. I was daydreaming." She sopped the spilled liquid with her napkin, glad for an excuse to temporarily avoid his laser gaze. "Is this an official visit? More background checks?"

He smiled then, a slow, easy grin that warmed her insides and made her instantly understand why the cove's single women looked at him cow-eyed.

"It's my day off," he said. "I'm out of uniform."

"You were out of uniform at my place last week,"

she quipped with a wobbly smile, vividly recalling his naked torso. "Didn't stop you from asking questions then."

"No questions, but I do have a warning."

"A warning?" Her guilty conscience slammed into overdrive.

"We've had several break-ins and some vandalism in the cove this past week. Be sure to keep your doors well-locked, even in the daytime."

"I always do. Force of habit for a city girl." She wondered if the recent break-ins had anything to do with the stranger Raylene had seen in town. "Any idea who's behind the trouble?"

When Dylan shrugged, she noted how broad his shoulders looked in the beige fisherman's sweater he wore over a dark brown turtleneck that matched his eyes and burnished hair, so thick she longed to run her fingers through it.

She mentally brought herself up short. She would *not* join the herd of besotted ladies of Casey's Cove, no matter how attractive Dylan Blackburn was. Besides, according to Raylene, with Jennifer's checkered past she definitely wasn't his type.

"Could be teenagers doing the break-ins," he said. "Or addicts looking for valuables to sell for drug money. Whoever it was wore gloves, so we haven't found any prints."

Dylan's news, coming on top of Raylene's information about the curious stranger, made Jennifer shiver. "I thought Casey's Cove was famous for its lack of crime."

"A string of incidents like these is unusual—" his

grin widened "—but, hey, if we had no crime at all, I'd be out of a job."

Raylene had appeared at Dylan's elbow with a mug and a coffeepot, poured Dylan a cup and was filling Jennifer's empty one.

"You could always help out Jarrett," the waitress said, apparently unembarrassed at eavesdropping. When Dylan declined to order, she moved to the next table.

"Jarrett?" Jennifer asked.

"My older brother. He inherited the family farm. It's about five miles up the valley."

"What does he raise?"

"Christmas trees."

Dylan sipped his coffee, and she couldn't help noticing the attractiveness of his long, slender fingers and spanking clean nails gripping the mug, making it seem small in his huge hands, hands that had her imagination spinning before she applied the brakes to her daydreams.

"Christmas trees are big business in this part of the state," he explained. "Would you like to see how they're grown?"

She couldn't risk spending too much time around Mr. Law-and-Order. "Maybe sometime—"

"How about today?"

"I can't. I promised Millie McGinnis I'd watch Sissy while Millie visits her sister at the hospital."

"We'll take Sissy, too. She'll enjoy the ride."

Jennifer waffled, knowing how much the little girl needed her thoughts diverted from her troubles. "I don't know—"

"Afterwards we'll drive out to Jack the Dipper's," Dylan said.

"Jack who?"

"It's the best ice-cream shop for fifty miles. Every little girl loves ice cream."

Jennifer felt herself weakening. She knew Sissy needed distracting from her mother's illness, and she feared bringing suspicion on herself if she made too big a point of evading the lawman's company.

"Christmas trees and ice cream," she acquiesced with a grin, hoping she wouldn't be sorry. "You sure know the way to a girl's heart."

"I have a couple of errands to run here in town, but they won't take long. Then we'll pick up Sissy."

"Sounds good." Once she had made up her mind to accept Dylan's offer, she was looking forward to it. Anything to keep from brooding over the stranger on her trail.

Dylan nodded at her barely-touched plate. "Finish your breakfast and I'll be right back."

Jennifer watched him cross the street to the police station, but she didn't touch her food. She doubted her appetite would revive any time soon. While she waited for Dylan to come back, she kept an eye on the street, on guard against the return of the black sport utility vehicle and the stranger with a picture that looked like her.

DYLAN LEANED BACK on the picnic bench, crossed his legs at the ankles, and watched Jennifer push Sissy on the park swing.

They'd had a busy day. First a visit with Jarrett at

the farm, where she'd fueled Jarrett's ego and earned his older brother's admiration with her questions about the Christmas tree business.

"What kinds of trees do you grow?" she'd asked.

"Scotch and Virginia pine and Leyland cypress." Jarrett pointed out examples of each species. "The cypress does best for us."

Jennifer inspected a tree carefully. "Do you have to shape them?"

Jarrett nodded. "We prune once or twice a year, depending on the species."

She eyed a tree that had grown to two feet above her head. "How old's this one?"

"Six years. It's ready for harvest."

She continued with more questions about fertilizers and irrigation. Jarrett was obviously impressed, and Dylan fleetingly wondered how a girl who'd lived all her life in the city of Memphis knew so much about farming.

When Jennifer had exhausted her questions and she and Sissy were gathering wildflowers between rows of immature trees, Jarrett grilled him about Jennifer.

"You serious about this one, little brother?"

Dylan reacted with surprise. "I barely know the woman."

Jarrett raised his eyebrows and cracked a grin. "And you're already bringing her home to meet the family? Sounds serious to me."

Dylan slugged Jarrett playfully on the shoulder. "You wouldn't know serious if it bit you. When's the last time you had a date?"

Jarrett shrugged. "You know how it is with farming—early to bed, early to rise and no let-up in between. Doesn't leave much time for a social life. However, if I'd met a girl like your Jennifer—"

"She's not *my* Jennifer."

"—I'd sure make the time. Don't let this one get away, bubba."

Unable to keep his older brother from jumping to conclusions, Dylan had simply shaken his head at his teasing.

After touring the farm, Dylan had taken Jennifer and Sissy to lunch in Sylva, followed by ice cream at Jack the Dipper's.

Now, in the late-afternoon sunshine, Sissy played happily at the park by the river, halfway home to Casey's Cove. The little girl shrieked with delight as Jennifer pushed the swing higher, and Jennifer's own merry laughter blended with the child's in a sound as pleasant as the river bubbling over its rocky bed.

Try as he might, Dylan couldn't reconcile the woman with whom he'd spent the day with the Jenny Thacker of his childhood memories. The young Jenny had been shy, reserved and aloof. Stuck-up, Tommy Bennett had called her. Maybe her inhibitions had been caused by the influence of the elderly aunt who had kept the girl under her thumb.

But *this* Jennifer was almost an exact opposite. As they'd tramped among the Scotch pines at the farm today, Dylan had found her outgoing, talkative, with an unlimited curiosity and a mischievous streak he would have never guessed resided in Jenny Thacker.

The girl and the woman she'd become were as opposite as ice and fire.

He watched as Jennifer grabbed Sissy out of the swing, whirled her around in her arms, then set her on her feet for a race to the riverbank. The two tossed stones at a quiet pool near the center of the river in the lee of a great boulder, and he noticed how Jennifer purposely shortened her throws so Sissy could win.

The woman was a miracle worker with children. He'd heard Miss Bessie lament that Sissy hadn't smiled since her mother entered the hospital, but today the girl had seemed genuinely happy in "Miss Jenny's" company and had laughed often.

As he observed the pair, Jennifer glanced toward the highway, visible from the park, and tensed as an oversized SUV sped past. He'd noticed her react that way several times that day to dark SUVs and wondered what she feared. In spite of her carefree attitude with Sissy, he caught an expression in her eyes every now and then when she didn't know he was watching, and he'd seen that look before.

Wary.

Frightened.

On guard.

She'd had that look in Raylene's Café this morning, and, in spite of her efforts to hide it, her hands had shaken.

A remnant of timid young Jenny Thacker? Or something more sinister? The woman was a puzzle, one he was curious to solve. It wasn't just his memories of that idyllic boyhood summer that drew him to her. He watched as she bent, grabbed a pebble and tossed it into the river with smooth, fluid movements. Fitted jeans, sneakers and a bulky sweater of hunter green did nothing to detract from the gracefulness of her slender figure. Her blond curls were wind-tossed, and her cheeks reddened by the chill of the late afternoon. Her green eyes sparkled with delight when Sissy's throw outdistanced her own, and her enticing lips rounded in a moue of surprise.

Kissable lips.

He jerked upright at the path his thoughts had taken. He hardly knew Jennifer Reid, even if he had kissed her once, almost twenty years ago. He doubted she'd forgive a second kiss as easily as the first. This Jennifer obviously knew her own mind, and if he intruded, seemed entirely capable of giving him a piece of it.

The setting sun slipped behind the mountains, and the air chilled suddenly. He shoved to his feet and walked down to the river's edge to join Jennifer and Sissy. "It's getting colder. We'd better head back."

Sissy, with her red curls, bright blue eyes, ruddy cheeks and impish expression, looked enough like Jennifer to be her daughter. She hefted the last pebble she'd gathered from the riverbank. "One more, please?"

"Okay," he relented. "Let's see how far you can throw."

Jennifer grinned, but her smile froze as she looked past him to the park entrance. He glanced back to see a black SUV turn into the parking area.

"You expecting someone?" he asked Jennifer.

She shook her head, as if coming out of a daze, but her eyes didn't leave the newly arrived vehicle until a couple of teenaged boys climbed out and headed to the open field, tossing a football between them.

Visibly relaxing, Jennifer turned her attention to Sissy. "Great throw. You could pitch for the Yankees."

"Not Yankees," the little Southerner said with a sour face.

Jennifer shrugged and acted as if she hadn't turned a ghostly white at the sight of the SUV a few seconds before. "Okay, then maybe the Atlanta Braves. That's some arm you have, kid."

"How about a piggyback?" Dylan knelt for Sissy to climb onto his back. "It's been a long day."

He carried the little girl to his pickup and strapped her into the child safety seat. Within minutes, the four-year-old was sound asleep.

"Shall I drop Sissy off at her Aunt Millie's?" He put the truck in gear and pulled onto the highway headed toward Casey's Cove.

Jennifer shook her head. "She's spending the night with me. Millie's going back to the hospital tomorrow, so I volunteered to keep Sissy the whole weekend."

They drove in silence for several miles through the dark shadows of trees that edged the highway, a narrow road that curved up the side of the mountain, with breathtaking vistas of the valley below before it edged downward into Casey's Cove.

Dylan hoped Jennifer would confide in him what

was frightening her. She didn't appear a naturally nervous type, and he figured whatever had spooked her might be serious. Her reactions that day had set his lawman's instincts on full alert. "Something you want to tell me?"

"Thanks for a wonderful day." She seemed to purposely misunderstand his question. "It's been great for Sissy, and I had a good time, too."

"You're welcome." With his inquiry squelched, he abandoned his questioning.

For now.

They continued in silence into Casey's Cove, along the dimly lit Main Street, quiet and deserted on a Saturday night, then headed up the mountain road on the other side of town toward Miss Bessie's guest house.

Jennifer gazed at the empty street as they passed. "What do folks do around here on Saturday night?"

"The townspeople are a pretty quiet bunch. Most of them stay at home, watch television, go to bed early for church tomorrow morning."

Jennifer sighed. "Isn't there anything to do for fun?"

Dylan glanced at her out of the corner of his eye. Little Jenny Thacker had definitely come out of her shell over the last twenty years. "There're a couple of places on the Sylva highway where you can get barbecue and dance to a jukebox. And there's a movie theater in town."

"Whew," she said with a smile, "all that excitement must be hard on the locals."

"We adapt." He turned the truck into the guest-house drive, climbed out and gently removed the sleeping Sissy from her carrier. "If you'll open the door, I'll bring her in."

He followed Jennifer into the house, through the living room and into the bedroom. She turned back the bedspread and blankets, and he laid the child on the bed. Tenderly, Jennifer removed Sissy's shoes and clothes, tugged on her nightgown, tucked her in and left a low light burning.

Back in the living room, Jennifer turned to him. "Would you like to stay for supper?"

"I don't want you going to any trouble."

"No trouble. Just grilled cheese sandwiches and soup."

He started to decline, then remembered how frightened she'd seemed at times during the afternoon. Maybe in the security of her own home, she'd let down her guard and tell him what she feared.

He decided to stay.

Chapter Three

"Soup and sandwiches sound good," he said. "Can I help?"

She grinned with the impishness he was growing fond of. "If you can open a can."

"I live alone, remember. Opening cans is my specialty."

He followed her into the kitchen and perched on a stool at the counter while she removed items from cupboards and the refrigerator.

"Do you like working for Miss Bessie?" he asked.

She nodded as she buttered bread for sandwiches. "I keep her books and the ones at the day-care center, and I also drive her wherever she wants to go. And yesterday we made apple butter for the festival next week." She paused, as if embarrassed by her chattering. "Anyway, working for her is more varied than the waitressing job I had in Nashville."

"Is that why you left Nashville?"

Wariness flashed briefly through the green depths of her eyes. She tugged slender fingers through a tumble of blond curls and avoided his gaze. "I was tired of waiting tables and wanted something different. Working for Miss Bessie's different all right.''

''So you'll be here for a while?''

She paused and looked at him. ''You ask an awful lot of questions.''

''Just friendly curiosity.'' He sensed the barriers going up around her. Unwilling to press further, he steered the conversation to neutral ground. ''So Miss Bessie's told you about the Apple Festival next week?''

''A little.'' She arranged thick slices of cheddar on the buttered bread, placed the sandwiches on a hot griddle, and handed him a can opener. With a few deft turns, he opened the vegetable gumbo and poured it into the saucepan she'd placed on the stove.

''The festival is the cove's biggest event of the year,'' he explained. ''Apples are the main crop here in the valley, and we have the maximum crowds of tourists the three days the festival runs.''

''Miss Bessie didn't tell me much about the festival except that she always wins the apple-butter competition.'' Jennifer turned the sandwiches on the griddle, and the aroma of toasting bread made his mouth water.

''There's the apple-pie bake-off, crowning the Apple Queen, a relay race where the runners have to carry an apple in a spoon...'' He stirred the soup as it came to a simmer, and she dropped in a handful of freshly chopped herbs. ''The Artisans' Hall has a special display of crafts, and Tommy Bennett's country band plays for the square-dancing and clogging exhibition.''

"Sounds like fun."

"More fun than the Fourth of July. You remember those celebrations?"

Her slight hesitation would have been lost on any-one not trained to observe as he was. Her glance slid away, avoiding him. "Oh, yeah, the fireworks off the pier. They were pretty spectacular."

Dylan lifted his eyebrows. "The fireworks were always fired from a barge in the middle of the lake."

"Right," she replied too quickly.

"You don't remember, do you?" Her lack of re-call disturbed him. She hadn't remembered his kiss, but even he had to admit that childish smack hadn't been as dazzling as the annual fireworks. He won-dered for an instant if she wasn't who she claimed to be, but thrust that unlikely notion aside. Miss Bes-sie would have seen through a phony at a hundred yards. Maybe Jennie Thacker has suffered from am-nesia, lost a portion of her life. Maybe she'd even returned to Casey's Cove to reclaim what was miss-ing.

He moved the soup off the burner, grasped her by the shoulders and turned her to face him. "Why don't you remember?" he asked gently.

Emotions flickered through her green eyes, and he recognized two predominant ones. Fear and shame. She looked so vulnerable, he wanted nothing more than to hold her close, to protect her from whatever demons lurked behind those fabulous eyes. He si-lently cursed himself for putting her on the spot. "It's none of my business—"

"No, it's okay." She took a deep breath, and he

felt the tension in her shoulders ease beneath his hands. "I'm just embarrassed—"

"Forget it. I was out of line."

"No problem." With a nod and a forgive-me smile, she shrugged out of his grasp and turned back to her sandwich preparations. She arranged the sandwiches and steaming soup bowls on a tray and handed it to him. "Why don't we eat in the living room in front of the fire?"

He carried the tray into the living room and placed it on a low table near the hearth. Jennifer touched a match to the kindling, and the logs caught quickly. Folding his legs beneath him, he sat on the floor.

With deft movements, she set a place mat in front of him, then his sandwich plate, soup bowl and flatware. She set her own place, sat cross-legged on the floor beside him and took a generous bite of sandwich. Neither whatever had frightened her earlier that day nor her recent embarrassment appeared to have had any effect on her appetite. In fact, her entire demeanor had relaxed as soon as he'd abandoned personal topics, which made him even more curious about her secrets.

Hungrier than he'd realized, he dug into his food. He could get used to this: a cozy supper shared with a beautiful woman in front of a glowing fire. The thought brought him up short. For the first time in almost two years, something warm and agreeable filled what had been a dark, empty vacuum. Not since Johnny Whitaker's untimely death had Dylan allowed himself to *feel* anything.

Jennifer Reid had changed all that.

"So—" she flicked a crumb from the corner of her mouth with a dainty swipe of her little finger "—how long have you been a cop?"

He knew she was leading the conversation away from herself, but he was in no hurry. He had the entire evening to discover what was frightening her.

"Almost twelve years," he said. "I went to the police academy right out of junior college."

"Have you always worked in Casey's Cove?" Her eyes sparkled with genuine interest, and he found her refreshing, a woman who seemed truly curious about him. Either that or she was purposely steering the conversation away from herself. Whatever her motive, he decided to humor her.

"Always. Never wanted to work anywhere else." He sipped his soup, found it remarkably tasty for a canned product and decided the difference had to be the fresh herbs Jennifer had added.

"Don't you ever get a hankering to travel, to see the rest of the world?" she asked.

He shook his head. "I'm a homebody. I've visited other places, but I'm always happy to return here. It's where I belong." He paused, then took a chance at a question of his own. "You didn't feel that way about Memphis?"

She laughed. "I've discovered I have an incurable wanderlust. I always want to be where I'm not. With no family or other ties, I'm free to go where I choose."

"So you'll be leaving here soon?" He watched her intently, gauging her reaction.

A hint of uncertainty flickered across the delicate

planes of her firelit face. "I don't know. Casey's Cove has a homey feel to it, but—"

She pushed to her feet, went into the kitchen and returned with the pan to fill his soup bowl. He accepted the refill with thanks and backed off his questions. She obviously wasn't ready to divulge any confidences.

When she had settled beside him again, she turned the conversation back to him. "What's the most memorable case you've ever worked?"

"It wasn't really *my* case, but it's one I can't forget." The emptiness yawned within him once again, threatening to suck him into its blackness. She must have noticed his change of mood, for her expression sobered.

"I'm sorry." She placed her hand on his sleeve, and he felt her warmth through his sweater, contrasting with the coldness inside him. "Looks like I touched a nerve."

He shook his head.

"If you'd rather not talk about it—"

He gathered his courage. "The department counselor says it's good for me to talk about it, if I can."

She nodded, her face veiled with compassion, and scooted so that her back rested against the front of the sofa. She didn't prod him, and her sympathetic presence eased his reluctance.

He shifted back against the sofa so that their shoulders touched, and he could feel the warm length of her against his body, comforting, easing the icy core that remembrance had formed deep inside him.

"Johnny Whitaker was my best friend," he began,

forming his words carefully, fearful he would lose control and break down in front of her. He sucked in a deep steadying breath and continued. "We grew up here in the cove together. His family lived up the mountain from our farm. His daddy made moonshine whiskey, and his older brothers were bootleggers. Johnny's mama was terrified of all of them. But not of Johnny."

Jennifer reached for his hand and laced her fingers through his, but said nothing to interrupt his story. He was grateful. If he stopped, he might not be able to begin again.

"Johnny might have turned out rotten like the rest of them if it hadn't been for Miss Bessie." He smiled, recalling the old woman's devotion. "When he was seven, Miss Bessie approached his mama and offered to send him to a boarding school in Asheville, but only on the condition that Johnny live with her on his holidays."

"His mother agreed?" Jennifer asked in surprise.

"Mrs. Whitaker was a good woman, God-fearing, but she feared the Whitaker men more. She wanted what was best for her youngest child, and she wanted him away from the bad influence of his father and brothers. As long as Miss Bessie allowed Mrs. Whitaker to visit Johnny on his holidays, his mama agreed. His father was glad to be rid of the boy. He was too young to work and just another mouth to feed."

A log burned through and crashed in the fireplace, sending a shower of sparks up the chimney. The only other sound in the room was the antique grandfather clock, ticking loudly in the corner.

"Johnny liked his boarding school. It was safe—his father couldn't beat him while he was there—and he had plenty to eat and a warm place to sleep. Not always the case at the Whitaker house. But his favorite time was school holidays." Dylan smiled. The pleasurable memories eased the grip of the icy center in his stomach. "We spent all our time together, fishing, swimming, picking blackberries."

"Sounds like an idyllic childhood," Jennifer murmured.

"It was. And when high-school graduation came, Johnny and I went to junior college together, and then the police academy. We came back to Casey's Cove and joined the department here. On our days off, we returned to the pursuits of our childhood. Things couldn't have been more perfect." Bitterness crept into his tone. "I should have realized at the time, things were *too* perfect."

She snuggled closer to him and slid her arm through his, and he was grateful for her nearness.

"Three years ago, numerous bombings of government buildings and facilities occurred in the southeast. Nothing on the scale of Oklahoma City, but deadly nonetheless. Several people were killed and millions of dollars in property were damaged."

"I remember. There was an explosion in Atlanta—" She broke off suddenly, as if sorry to have interrupted.

"They were terrible, but like so many things, the bombings didn't seem real here in the cove, just something that we saw on the evening news that didn't touch us.''

He shivered violently, an involuntary shudder. ''We had no idea how close to home it all really was.

''For several weeks after the last bombings, news reports kept announcing that the FBI and ATF had no clues to the identities of the perpetrators. Then one October day two years ago, a group of FBI and AFT agents arrived in Casey's Cove. A witness had spotted someone at the scene of the last bombing before the explosion occurred. The witness worked with an artist to produce a composite sketch, and the computer tentatively matched the sketch to Johnny Whitaker's dad.''

''Oh, no.'' She gripped his arm tighter against her.

''I confronted Johnny, asked him if he knew whether his dad or brothers were involved in the militant group that had committed the bombings. He swore he knew nothing about it, that there had to have been a mistake, that his dad and brothers were into illegal moonshining, but not bombings.'' He drew a long rattling breath. ''I made Johnny promise to tell me, to tell the FBI if he found out otherwise. He promised.''

She shifted uneasily beside him as if she'd picked up a glimmering of where his story was headed.

''The federal agents didn't wait for word from Johnny. They decided to move on the Whitaker place immediately. I looked for Johnny at his place to warn him, but couldn't find him. I was asked to accompany the feds as the local liaison officer, and we headed into the hills.

"The Whitaker men were waiting for us, and opened fire immediately. Suddenly Johnny appeared out of nowhere, screaming for them to stop shooting so he could rescue his mother. He was out of uniform, and the feds didn't recognize him—except for his strong family resemblance to the other Whitaker men."

His words died in his throat, and his pulse pounded in his ears. He could hear again the screams and the rattle of gunfire, smell the acrid stench of cordite, see the blood and Johnny's sightless eyes staring at the cloudless blue of the Carolina sky while Dylan held his hand as he died.

He stopped, unable to go on. The ticks of the clock thundered in the silence. Jennifer didn't move.

After several minutes, Dylan continued. "Mrs. Whitaker and Johnny were both killed in the cross fire. Whitaker and his older sons were captured, tried and convicted. They're all serving life terms in federal prison."

He shook his head, overwhelmed with a sadness he would never lose. "If Johnny hadn't lied to me about his family's involvement—if I'd known the truth, maybe I could have worked out a plan that would have saved Mrs. Whitaker and spared Johnny."

"It wasn't your fault—"

"I was there when it happened, and there was nothing I could do to stop it."

"Johnny made his choice, for whatever reason. Maybe he thought he was protecting his mother.

Maybe he had a plan of his own he didn't have time to carry out.''

He hung his head and bit back tears. "But I'll never know for sure. All I know is that my best friend lied to me, and now he's dead."

He felt her move beside him, and in an instant she had settled on his lap with her arms around him, drawing him close in the warmth of her embrace. He yielded to her caress, buried his face in the hollow of her neck, absorbed her heat and used her supple body as a shield against the numbing coldness that enveloped him. The fragrance of honeysuckle scattered the vestiges of gun smoke and blood from his memory. His muscles relaxed. His breathing slowed.

He didn't know how long they held each other. The clock struck the quarter, then the half hour, and still they didn't move. Then, gently, she drew back, placed her hands on either side of his face and raised her lips to his. Her kiss at first was comforting, succor to his pain, blissful alleviation of the hollow ache in his soul.

She tasted of sweet herbs and honey, and her scent infused his senses. Her soothing warmth turned to heat, her tender touch to electricity. He wrapped his arms around her and pulled her closer, savoring the taste of her, the weight of her in his arms. His heart thudded with excitement, and he could feel her heartbeats pounding beneath the softness of her breasts pressed against his chest.

Suffused with sudden desire, he slid his hands beneath her sweater and felt the heat of her bare skin against his palms, but his touch apparently broke the trance between them, and she pulled away.

The green of her eyes was smoky with desire, her lips reminded him of a bruised blossom and high color stained her cheeks, but he couldn't read the expression on her face.

"Maybe I should apologize," he offered, "but I won't say I'm sorry."

Unexpectedly, she threw back her head and laughed. "No need for an apology. Not unless that kiss was another bet with Tommy Bennett."

"No way," he said. "And no way was that kiss anything like our first one."

She seemed agitated then, as if in stating there'd been two, he was implying there might be more. She jumped to her feet. "I'd better check on Sissy."

He heard her rush into the bedroom, then heard the bathroom door close behind her. He probably shouldn't have kissed her. Not like that. She'd only been showing sympathy, and he'd wanted more.

Dumb move.

But he'd learned a long time ago—and the hard way—that things already done could not be undone and had to be dealt with. With a sigh, he stacked the dirty dishes on the tray and carried them into the kitchen.

When she returned from the bathroom a short time later, hair combed, face scrubbed and fresh lipstick applied, he had almost finished the washing-up.

As if nothing unusual had transpired between them, she took a clean towel from a drawer, removed a soup bowl from the drain rack and began wiping it dry. "Sissy's sound asleep."

He nodded, dried his hands. "Guess I'd better shove off then."

She hesitated, as if debating whether to ask him to stay. He hoped she would. He still hadn't learned what caused the fear that flitted across her face when she was unaware he was watching.

Then, as if making up her mind, she nodded. "I'll see you to the door."

A few minutes later, he was cruising through Casey's Cove on his way home. He wasn't sorry he'd shared Johnny's story with her, and he damned well wasn't sorry he'd kissed her.

What he *did* regret was that he hadn't kissed her again when he'd left, but her barriers had gone up once more, effectively closing off any advances on his part.

With a sigh, he turned into the driveway, parked in front of his dark and empty house and went inside to his lonely bed.

JENNIFER DIDN'T SLEEP that night. She lay awake, listening to the moaning wind and the clickety-clack of dry leaves scuttling across the roof, and wondering what to do next.

Her biggest dilemma was the mysterious stranger who had queried Raylene at the café. If the man had any inkling Jennifer was staying in Casey's Cove, she wasn't safe and needed to find a new hiding place immediately. A part of her urged her to get up, pack and flee as fast as she could.

But another part urged patience. The man might have believed Raylene and moved on, never to return to Casey's Cove again. In that case, if she decided to stay put for a while, she was free to remain with Miss Bessie and Sissy, both of whom she'd grown fond of in the few short days she'd spent with them.

And she'd grown fond of Dylan Blackburn.

Too fond.

If she could have kicked herself lying down, she would have. She'd only meant to comfort him with her kiss, but it had turned into something much more than solace. She'd never responded with such intensity to any man, and it had taken all her self-restraint to break away. If she remained in Casey's Cove, she'd see Dylan again. She'd kiss him again. Then he'd ask more questions that she couldn't answer, and she would wish she hadn't stayed.

As the sun crept over the mountain behind Miss Bessie's mansion, Jennifer tossed in the massive Edwardian carved oak bed and socked her pillow. She should leave, but she *wanted* to stay, wanted a home, friends, family.

A life.

But her life was exactly what she might lose if she remained where the man on her trail could find her.

A high-pitched giggle at the foot of the bed snapped her out of her internal debate. Sissy McGinnis, barefooted and wearing a sunny yellow nightshirt, peered over the edge of the mattress, her blue eyes wide with laughter.

"Good morning, sunshine," Jennifer greeted her.

"Hi." The little girl turned suddenly shy.

"Are you hungry?"

Sissy nodded, and Jennifer reached down and swooped the child into her arms and under the covers. "How about breakfast at Raylene's, and then I'll read you the funny papers before time for Sunday school?"

"Can I have pancakes?"

Jennifer hugged the girl close. How could she leave Sissy now, when the child had just come to trust her? Sissy had already been traumatized by her mother's hospitalization. Jennifer's desertion would only add to that hurt.

"You can have all the pancakes you want," she promised. "Now you stay here where it's warm while I turn up the heat and run your bath."

A couple of hours later, Jennifer, with Sissy beside her, sat in her favorite booth at Raylene's, reading the *Peanuts* comic strip to the little girl.

Sissy laughed. "I like Snoopy. I wish I had a doggie."

Raylene had already cleared their dishes. Now she slid the check toward Jennifer. "Nice to see you laughing again, Sissy McGinnis. You having a good time?"

Sissy nodded. "I spent the night with Miss Jenny."

Raylene grinned. "Looks like you got your appetite back, too. You ate three of Grover's blueberry pancakes."

"Be sure to thank him for me," Jennifer said. "Not every little girl gets pancakes shaped like Mickey Mouse."

"You're one of Grover's favorites," Raylene said, "and Sissy, too."

"Raylene?"

"Need something else?"

Jennifer shook her head. "I was just wondering if you'd seen that tough-looking guy again, the one with the picture that looked like me?"

Raylene shook her head and gave Jennifer a probing look. "You sure you don't know him?"

"Pretty sure. But will you let me know if he shows up again? Maybe I'll track him down and make sure he's no one I'm acquainted with."

Jennifer didn't like lying. Even worse, she didn't like Raylene obviously *knowing* she was lying. But at least she'd asked the waitress to give her a head's up in case the stranger showed up again in Casey's Cove.

In case she decided to stay.

The peal of bells at the Baptist church, a white frame building on the promontory by the marina, broke through the morning quiet.

"Time for Sunday school, Sissy," Jennifer said, glad for an excuse to end her discussion of the stranger. "Miss Bessie will be waiting for us."

They attended Miss Bessie's Sunday-school class for pre-school girls, and after church drove the old woman home and joined her for Sunday dinner. Later, Jennifer and Miss Bessie sat in rockers on the wide front porch overlooking the valley, while Sissy curled up for a nap in the porch swing.

"I understand you and Sissy spent the day with Dylan Blackburn yesterday," Miss Bessie said.

Jennifer wasn't surprised. Not much went on in Casey's Cove that Miss Bessie didn't know about. She filled her employer in on the details of her Saturday, omitting only Dylan's story of his best friend's death.

And the kiss she'd shared with Dylan.

"Must have done him a world of good," Miss Bessie said with a firm shake of her white curls.

"What?" Jennifer, still thinking of Dylan's kiss, blushed.

"You saw Dylan in church this morning?"

Jennifer nodded. He'd looked even more handsome than she remembered with the morning sun streaming through the tall Gothic window, burnishing his thick brown hair with a sheen of gold. They had nodded to each other and smiled when he entered, but she hadn't talked with him.

"It's the first time Dylan's set foot in church since Johnny Whitaker's funeral," Miss Bessie said. "Ever since that poor boy died, Dylan's cut himself off from people. Oh, he does his job. He's too conscientious not to, but his heart hasn't been in it. But this morning when I spoke with him after the service, he seemed almost like his old self."

Jennifer had ducked out a side door after church, telling herself it was the quickest way to pick up Sissy in the nursery, but she'd really been avoiding running into Dylan. How could she decide whether to leave Casey's Cove when she felt irresistibly drawn to a police officer, someone she should avoid like the plague?

Throughout Miss Bessie's fried-chicken dinner,

served by Estelle, the housekeeper, Jennifer had continued her internal debate. She had finally concluded her safest bet was to hit the road, and she was working up her courage to tell Miss Bessie she'd be moving on.

"My dear," Miss Bessie continued, "I don't know how to thank you."

"For what?" Jennifer had been so lost in her own thoughts, she'd almost forgotten the elderly woman beside her.

"You've saved my life," Miss Bessie said. "Until you arrived, I'd about given up. For the first time in my life, I was feeling *old* and worthless. But with your help, your youth and enthusiasm, I feel now like I'm good for another decade."

"You'll never be worthless to the people in this community, Miss Bessie, not with all you've done for them all your life."

"But I had just about stopped doing," Miss Bessie said with a wave of age-spotted hands. "But now, with you to help me, I can continue the work my father started here a hundred years ago."

Jennifer swallowed hard. She couldn't tell Miss Bessie she was leaving now, not after the woman's impassioned speech of gratitude. "I enjoy working for you," she admitted, knowing she spoke the truth.

"Good, because this coming week, with the Apple Festival approaching, I'm going to need more help than ever. First, you'll need to supervise the construction of the booth where I sell my apple butter...."

Jennifer nodded dutifully to the long list of instructions, feeling torn between wanting to remain in the cove where she had been so readily accepted and wanting to flee the man who followed her. Maybe she could find someone else to help Miss Bessie, so she could make her getaway.

With a stretch and a yawn, Sissy woke from her nap and sat up in the swing. Jennifer glanced at her watch. "Ready to go see Aunt Millie, sunshine?"

Sissy nodded, and Jennifer gathered the child in her arms. "May I keep the car, Miss Bessie? I thought I'd take in a movie tonight."

"Of course, dear. If I need anything, Estelle can drive me."

Jennifer dropped Sissy off at her aunt's, then continued down the highway toward Sylva. She grabbed a quick sandwich at a fast-food drive-through, then headed for the shopping complex where the theater was located. She was hoping a good movie would distract her from the back-and-forth argument going on in her head. She wasn't any closer to making a decision, and the internal debate was wearing her out.

The movie, a romantic comedy, helped her relax— too much. Five minutes after the opening credits, she was sound asleep. She didn't waken until the lights came on and the music soared when the movie ended.

Feeling groggy and disoriented, she hurried to her car. She was glad to see that the night was clear. Crossing the mountains with their narrow two-lane roads full of serpentine curves, switchbacks and narrow shoulders the only thing between the car and a steep drop was bad enough on a clear night. On a foggy night, the trip was close to suicide.

The traffic faded outside Sylva, and hers was the only car on the narrow road—

Until she crossed the gap where the road wound up the mountain toward Casey's Cove.

Headlights appeared behind her, riding her bumper. She increased her speed as much as she could, but with most of the curves posting fifteen-mile-an-hour limits, she wasn't willing to risk her life to satisfy the impatient driver behind her.

She couldn't get her bearings very well in the darkness, but she was fairly certain there was no place for the car to pass her before she crested the mountain.

Doggedly maintaining her speed and adjusting her rearview mirror to keep the headlights from blinding her, she held the Mercedes on the road.

Suddenly, her car jolted. The driver behind her had tapped her bumper. She hit the accelerator only to slam on the brakes at the approach of a hairpin turn. The car behind her hit her again.

Thoroughly frightened, alone on the mountain road with no sign of other cars and only steep acres of forest on one side and dizzying cliffs on the other, she prayed the crazy driver behind her would wait until she could find a place to pull over and then pass and leave her alone.

She shifted into second gear and started up another incline. As she reached the peak of the hill, she could see the valley below, scattered with lights from farms and other buildings. Near the continental divide, the altitude was almost a mile high, and the drop from the road to the valley below at least half that distance.

Her palms sweated and slipped on the wheel. She dried one hand at a time on her jeans, then gripped the wheel, hoping the car behind wouldn't shove her off the road and send her soaring into the valley below.

Suddenly the car pulled out from behind her and raced alongside. Afraid to take her eyes off the treacherous road ahead, she didn't look at it. With luck, it would pass her before another car rounded the curve and hit them head on. And when it did, she'd memorize the license plate and report the maniac to Dylan Blackburn.

The other car slowed slightly, throwing its headlights into her outside rearview mirror and almost blinding her. She heard its engine rev, and it was beside her again.

With a sudden twist of the wheel, the unknown driver rammed her front left fender with his car, knocking the Mercedes onto the gravel surface of the shoulder. Her tires spun on the loose rock, and she fought the wheel to get the car back on the asphalt.

Dear God, was he trying to kill her?

She thought immediately of Raylene's stranger and feared he had found her. What better way to silence her than to kill her in a car crash?

With a vicious twist of the steering wheel, the vehicle beside her struck her again, forcing her off the road.

Before Jennifer could react, she felt the Mercedes go airborne. A scream ripped from her throat.

She was barely aware of the impact before her world went black.

Chapter Four

Dylan had just turned off the late news when his phone rang.

"Dylan," Phyllis Dayton, the weekend dispatcher said. "Sorry to bother you on your night off, but we have a bad accident on the main highway. The boys could sure use your help."

"On my way." Dylan grabbed his keys and jacket and headed out the door, happy for a distraction from persistent thoughts of Jennifer Reid. He couldn't understand why she affected him so strongly. Surely he wasn't that enamored of a childhood dream. And he'd known plenty of other pretty women—but, he admitted grudgingly, none of them had touched his spirit the way Jennifer had. He wanted to spend more time with her, to kiss her again, more than that, to—

He wrenched his thoughts from the provocative woman and turned them toward the dispatcher's call. He hoped no one had been injured in the wreck.

Bad, Phyllis had said, a euphemism the department and the news media sometimes employed when fatalities had occurred. He climbed into his pickup and stomped the gas, roaring through the sleeping town and heading up the incline to Bald Gap.

The strobing red lights of the Jackson County rescue trucks flickering through the trees on the switchback above announced the accident site long before his arrival. When he reached the scene, deputies had the road blocked in both directions, and paramedics were unloading equipment.

Only one thing was missing. The wreck.

"Where're the cars?" He approached the deputy and flashed his Casey's Cove Police Department ID.

"Only one," the grim-faced deputy replied. "It's over the side."

"Survivors?"

The deputy shrugged. "Won't know till we reach them. And that may take a while."

Dylan approached the narrow shoulder of the road and noticed another vehicle parked back from the rescue van. Ben Morgan, looking green around the gills, slouched against the side of his late-model gray Cadillac. He raised his head, saw Dylan and managed a feeble wave.

Dylan joined him. "You okay?"

The Realtor pushed shaking fingers through his silver hair. "Paramedic says my blood pressure's spiked, but that's to be expected. I arrived just after the car went over the side. Called 911 on my cell phone. Can't say I was totally surprised, though."

Dylan jerked his head toward the ravine where the car rested. "Were they speeding?"

Ben shook his head. "Not that I know of. But the

darn fool teenagers who passed me earlier and almost ran me off the road were driving like bats outta hell.''

"You think it's one of them?" Dylan asked.

"The teenagers were in pickups. The car down there's a Mercedes."

"Mercedes?" Dylan rushed to the edge of the overlook and peered into the darkness. Miss Bessie Shuford owned a Mercedes, but so did a dozen or more seasonal visitors to the area. As he looked, a rescue worker switched on emergency lighting that illuminated the area below, and Dylan recognized the vehicle by its color and tag. "Good God, it's Miss Bessie's car."

Ben Morgan joined him. "Miss Bessie wouldn't be driving. She suffers from night blindness."

Dylan glimpsed a tumble of blond curls pressed between the inflated air bags and the driver's window, and his heart stopped. "It's Jennifer Reid, Miss Bessie's assistant. And Miss Bessie could be with her."

"I can find out quick enough." Ben jogged back to his car and picked up his cell phone.

Dylan sprinted to the rescue van. "What's the holdup on getting them out of there?"

The paramedic, Gary Patterson, a native of Casey's Cove, was assembling a harness and rope, rappelling equipment. "Good news is the car struck that shelf twenty feet down from the road. That kept it from plunging all the way into the valley."

"And the bad news?"

"There's one old hickory holding that Mercedes from going over the edge. The trunk's about rotted through, and one wrong move could bust that car loose and send it flying. We've only got so much time before gravity pulls it over the edge.''

"I'm trained for mountain rescue," Dylan said. "Got another harness?"

Patterson handed Dylan a set of equipment, and as he donned the harness, Ben Morgan approached.

"Talked to Miss Bessie," he said. "As far as she knows, Jennifer is alone in the car."

"Thanks." Dylan looked to the paramedic. "It'll make it easier with only one to rescue. You ready?"

The paramedic nodded. The two men secured their lines at the top of the cliff and rappelled down the rock face to the ledge where the Mercedes teetered precariously.

Although it was less than twenty feet from the road to the shelf, to Dylan it felt like hundreds and seemed to take forever to descend. With every push off the rocky cliff wall, he thought of Jennifer Reid with her tousled blond curls, impish smile and compassionate heart. He refused to believe someone so vibrant and spirited could be dead. With all his strength, he willed her to survive and rejected any other possibility.

Finally his feet hit the ledge, and he edged his way toward the driver's door. The rotten wood in the trunk of the ancient hickory splintered and cracked, sounding like gunshots echoing across the dark valley.

"It's slipping," Patterson yelled.

Dylan lunged for the door handle, and the car shifted slightly. Rocks spun from beneath the tires and fell into the abyss, so far below he couldn't hear them hit bottom.

"Careful," Patterson called. "It can take you over the side with it."

Dylan signaled his acknowledgement, but his attention was focused on the blond curls visible through the window. For an instant, he thought he saw movement.

The Mercedes shifted again, sliding closer to the edge.

Dylan waited only a millisecond before hastening into action. With one swooping movement, he yanked open the door, pushed away the side air bag, and unfastened the seat belt. He scooped Jennifer into his arms and jumped back from the car—just as the hickory trunk gave way and the Mercedes followed it over the edge.

Breathing heavily, shaken by their near brush with death, Dylan cradled Jennifer in his arms, grateful for the warmth seeping through her clothes that indicated she was still alive. He'd covered dozens of accidents in his years as a cop, but this one was different. At the sight of the injured woman in his arms, he felt his objectivity slipping away and panic threatening to set in. He took a deep breath. The best way to help Jennifer was to remain professional. Calm and detached.

The paramedic approached and checked her over while Dylan held her, all three flattened against the cliffside to keep from pitching off the mountain into the darkness below.

"Vital signs are weak," the medic said, "and she

has a concussion, probably caused by that gash on her head.''

Rescuers above lowered a stretcher, and Dylan and Patterson strapped the unconscious Jennifer to it. The only relief from the stark white of her face was the nasty welt on her forehead, a smattering of freckles across the bridge of her nose and the dark smudge of her eyelashes against her pale cheeks. More than anything, Dylan wanted her to open those magnificent green eyes and assure him she was all right, but she lay so still, he feared for her survival.

''Haul her up,'' he shouted.

Within minutes, deputies and paramedics above pulled the stretcher up the rock face and lifted it onto the road. They were loading Jennifer into the rescue van when Dylan and Patterson climbed over the edge of the cliff onto the narrow shoulder.

Patterson climbed inside, and with a scream of sirens, the van started immediately toward Sylva and the hospital. Dylan checked with the deputy in charge to see if he was still needed, then jumped into his pickup and followed the ambulance toward town.

SHE WAS FALLING...*falling*....

Jennifer awoke with a jerk.

''Whoa, take it easy.'' Dylan Blackburn stood beside her bed and pressed her back against the pillows with firm but gentle hands.

Sunlight poured through a window half-shuttered with mini-blinds. From outside the unfamiliar pastel-colored room came the sounds of hushed voices and muted footsteps.

The last thing she remembered was soaring off the road into the darkness, believing she was going to die.

Now, standing beside her, Dylan looked like an angel, backlit by sunlight from the window behind him. Was she dead? Had she gone to Heaven? And if so, what was Dylan doing there?

"Where am I?" she asked.

"The hospital in Sylva. You're going to be fine."

As he leaned closer and her vision focused, she noted the stubble on his chin and cheeks and the dark circles under his eyes.

"What about you?" she asked. "You look terrible. Are you okay?"

"He's fine, but he won't go home and rest like the doctor told him to." A stranger, dressed in a paramedic's uniform, stood in the doorway.

Dylan motioned the paramedic into the room. "Jennifer, meet Gary Patterson. He helped me pull you from the wreck—"

"Oh, no!" Realization flooded through her. She tried to sit up, but was too weak, and collapsed onto her pillow. "Miss Bessie's car!"

"No need to fret," Dylan said. "Miss Bessie was here earlier to check on you. The Mercedes is fully insured, and she said you're not to worry about it."

"You're a lucky lady," Patterson said. "If Dylan hadn't grabbed you when he did, you'd be at the bottom of the ravine with what's left of that Mercedes."

She turned to Dylan. "You saved my life?"

He shrugged, obviously embarrassed by Patterson's praise. "To protect and serve. That's my job. Besides, Patterson did more. He brought you here in good condition."

Patterson smiled. "Just wanted to see how you were doing, Ms. Reid, before I start my shift. Do what the doctors order and you'll be out of here in no time."

He hurried out the door before she could thank him. Dylan dragged a chair beside the bed, turned it backwards and straddled it with his arms folded on the backrest. She squirmed under his intense scrutiny.

"Am I under arrest or something?" she asked.

His eyes widened. "Why do you say that?"

"Do they place every patient here under police guard?"

He shook his head. "You're not under guard. I…just wanted to make sure you were okay, and that you didn't wake up alone."

Her eyes teared at his thoughtfulness. "You didn't have to—"

"I wanted to. You almost died out there last night."

The dark memories she'd been holding at bay suddenly inundated her. She drew a long, shuddering breath, remembering.

"What happened?" Dylan asked.

"I'm not sure. One minute I was alone on the highway, the next there was a car on my bumper. It hit my car, trying to get me to speed up, I guess. Then it tried to pass. It forced me off the road." She held back her theory of Raylene's stranger trying to kill her. That piece of information would invite questions she was unwilling to answer.

"Can you describe the car or the driver?" His inquiry was gentle, but she could hear the steel in his voice. She'd never want to be a criminal with Dylan Blackburn on her trail. The thought made her shiver.

He must have noticed her reaction, for he rose, grabbed a blanket folded at the foot of her bed and tucked it tenderly around her. "Better?"

She nodded, but her coldness wasn't caused by the temperature. She couldn't help but wonder if the stranger in the black SUV had tracked her down, followed her from Sylva last night and forced her off the mountain.

Dead women tell no tales.

"I couldn't see the car or the driver. The headlights blinded me."

He patted her hand. "Don't worry. Ben Morgan was on the road not far behind you. He got a good look at the suspects and their vehicles, and the sheriff's department picked them up this afternoon."

She was afraid to ask the next question, but she had to know. "Who were they?"

"Couple of drag-racing teenagers from the university. In his zeal to win, one of them must have forced you off the road."

She fell back against the pillow in relief. "Teenagers?"

Dylan nodded, his jaw set, his eyes hard. "They almost killed you. And it'll take days to retrieve the Mercedes from the bottom of the ravine."

"You're sure it was them?"

He hesitated. "They swear they didn't pass anyone except Ben Morgan in his Cadillac, but they could be lying to save their own hides. According to folks who live along the highway, there wasn't anyone else on the road at the time."

Her shivering eased. She was safe. It hadn't been Raylene's mysterious stranger set on murder, but a horrible accident. She'd have to consider all her options, but *maybe* she could remain safely in Casey's Cove after all.

She looked at Dylan, his handsome face lined with fatigue, and felt suddenly guilty. "Have you been here all day?"

"Since they brought you in last night." He sloughed off her question as if his presence was no big deal, but his obvious concern for her gladdened her heart.

She reached for his hand. "You saved my life, then kept watch over me. I don't know how to thank you."

"No thanks necessary." He grinned, with a warmth that banished the tiredness around his eyes, and squeezed her fingers gently. "Just get better so you can break out of this joint."

"On one condition."

He raised an eyebrow and cast her a roguish head-to-toe glance. "Doesn't look like you're in a position to bargain."

"Then think of it as a favor."

"I can seldom resist doing favors for pretty ladies."

"Now you're being chivalrous," she said with a

laugh. "Thank God there's no mirror in this room. I can only imagine what I must look like." If her face looked as bad as it felt, it had to be black and blue.

The mahogany brown of his eyes darkened dangerously, and when he spoke, his deep voice was husky with emotion. "You look just fine to me."

Flustered, she broke away from the intensity of his gaze. "It's you I'm worried about. You need a warm bath, a hot meal and a good night's sleep, or they'll be checking you in here, too."

His magnificent eyes twinkled with mischief. "Maybe we could share a bed."

"I may have cracked my head, but I haven't lost my senses." She pretended outrage, but was surprised at how appealing she found his suggestion, the idea of lying sheltered in his arms.

He bent over her and cupped her cheek in his big, strong hand. In spite of herself, she leaned into his touch, reveling in how safe he made her feel, surprised by the stirring of her senses.

"The doctor says you can go home tomorrow." He drew closer and brushed his lips against hers, the merest flutter of a kiss that sent lightning spiraling through her. "I'll see you then."

Breathless, she watched him leave, keenly aware of his absence before his shadow cleared the door.

Rubbing her lips still warm from his kiss, she lay back on her pillow and tried to assess her situation. From Dylan's explanation, her accident hadn't been an intended hit by Raylene's mysterious stranger, but the careless result of teenage daredevils. Should she count herself lucky and flee Casey's Cove while the coast was clear?

Or should she indulge herself and remain with her new friends who had come to mean so much to her?

Too much, in the case of Dylan Blackburn.

Every ounce of common sense she possessed screamed at her to avoid further contact with a lawman whose keen eyes and sharp intuition missed nothing, a man who hated liars and the damage their lies caused, an irresistably attractive man who threatened to make her forget her resolutions not to get involved emotionally.

Again she brushed her hand across her lips, still tingling from Dylan's kiss. Her heart effectively squelched her common sense. Looking forward to seeing him again tomorrow, she closed her eyes and fell asleep.

DYLAN FINISHED his Tuesday shift at three o'clock, changed clothes in the station locker room, and headed up the mountain to Miss Bessie's, anxious to see Jennifer again. He found her, ensconced in pillows on the chaise longue on the front porch. Spots of high color on her cheekbones relieved the former pallor of her face, and her extraordinary green eyes brightened at the sight of him, making his pulse beat faster. Only a thin red welt on her forehead and a dark bruise on her jaw remained as visible souvenirs of her accident.

"Feeling better?" he asked.

She seemed happy to see him, and he marveled at how good her reaction made him feel.

"Ben Morgan drove me home this morning," she said, "but Miss Bessie refuses to let me stay alone at the guest house. She insists that she and Estelle take care of me."

He nodded toward the table beside her. "Looks like she's keeping her word."

She glanced at the table, laden with a pitcher of lemonade, a plate piled high with the infamous cinnamon rolls, the latest mystery novel and a massive bouquet of purple Joe Pye weed, goldenrod and frothy white Queen Anne's lace.

"Would you like a drink?" she asked.

He accepted the lemonade and declined the cinnamon rolls.

"Please, can't you take some back to the station with you?" she begged in a whisper. "I can't eat them."

"Nobody can," Dylan said with a laugh, but he took pity on her and wrapped several rolls in a paper napkin to dispose of later.

"Now you've saved my life twice," she said with a dazzling smile that made his knees weak.

He sank into a rocker beside her. "Any aftereffects from your accident?"

She shook her head. "Not even a headache. But I'll die of boredom if Miss Bessie and Estelle don't let me up soon."

"What did the doctor say?"

"To use my own judgment. I feel *fine,* but Miss Bessie's adamant about keeping me quiet."

"How about a drive?" he suggested. "I can take

you down to the elementary school. They've started preparations for the festival.''

''Please,'' she begged with a rueful smile, ''but you'll have to convince Miss Bessie first.''

Whatever latent fear he'd seen in Jennifer's eyes the first few days had disappeared, and he wondered at its absence. Maybe he'd misread her initially, and it hadn't been fear at all, but a residue of the natural shyness she'd exhibited as a child. Or maybe she'd overcome the demons that had hounded her. Whatever the reason, he was happy to see her at ease and looked forward to spending more time with her. More than spend time, he wanted to hold her, to kiss her again. He'd known she was special that long ago summer. She was more than special now.

He found Miss Bessie in the kitchen, stirring up another batch of her famous apple butter which, unlike her cinnamon rolls, was a favorite in the cove. The rich, spicy aroma made him hungry.

She turned from the stove as he entered, and he suppressed a smile at the sight of the tiny woman covered chin to toe in a voluminous pinafore apron hand-stitched from cotton feedsacks. A pair of white sneakers tied with day-glo green laces peaked from beneath the hem.

''Come to take my patient off my hands?'' she asked.

He grinned. ''You're sharp, Miss Bessie. I can't slide anything by you. Thought I'd drive Jennifer down to the elementary school and show her the festival site.''

''Good idea. She'll be manning my apple-butter

booth if she's up to it." She gave her concoction a final stir, dropped the large spoon into the sink and wiped her hands on the front of her apron. "The insurance adjuster called this morning. Wants to know how long before my car's retrieved from the bottom of the ravine."

"I talked with George Spivey, the salvager, this morning. He says he'll have it out by Thursday. The adjuster can inspect it at Spivey's garage anytime after that."

"Thanks," Miss Bessie said. "I'll let him know. And, Dylan?"

"Yes?"

"Jennifer's had quite a shock from her ordeal. Don't you go getting her overly excited."

"I doubt the festival site will stir her up that much," he said wryly.

"I may be older than dirt," the elderly woman said with a sparkle in her blue eyes, "but I'm not blind. I saw the way you looked at her in the hospital, and you know exactly what I'm talking about."

Dylan shook his head. "Miss Bessie, you've been standing over a hot stove too long. I think it's cooked your brain."

"You young scamp!" She flapped her apron at him. "Get on with your courting and leave me to my work."

With a wink and a nod, he left Miss Bessie in her kitchen and returned to Jennifer on the porch. He'd have to be careful. If his feelings were so apparent to Miss Bessie, they might be equally obvious to Jennifer, and he had no intention of making a fool of himself over any woman.

But his good intentions dissipated when Jennifer stood to accompany him, and her knees gave way. With a fluid movement, he swept her into his arms. "I'll carry you to the car."

She flushed with embarrassment. "I'm sorry—"

"Staying in bed too long ruins your muscle tone," he said breezily, trying not to show how powerfully her proximity affected him. Her honeysuckle fragrance tickled his nose, her breath warmed his cheek and her body felt feather-light in his arms. "You'll regain it soon enough."

The walk to the pickup seemed too short, and he regretted having to release her when he placed her in the passenger seat. He climbed into the driver's seat and eased the truck down the steep drive.

"Need anything here?" he asked as they passed the guest house.

"Not now. Maybe we could stop on the way back."

He continued down the mountain and glanced over to find her staring at him, eyes clouded with worry. "Something on your mind?"

"Those boys, the ones who hit me. What will happen to them?"

"They've been arraigned, and they're free on bail for now. I suppose they're back in class at the university."

"Will I have to be a witness at their trial?" Apprehension edged her voice, but he didn't find that unusual. Even innocent people were often intimidated by the awesome workings of the court system.

"Unless the prosecutor works out a plea bargain. They could spend years in prison for their carelessness."

"Years?"

"Ten to twenty. They're lucky they're not charged with vehicular homicide." Bitterness laced his voice, but he couldn't help it. He had no use for people who endangered the lives of others. And only by the grace of God and incredible luck had Jennifer survived that crash. He'd been glad the Jackson County deputies, not he, had been the arresting officers. He didn't believe in police brutality, but he would have had a hard time remaining objective in this case.

Realization suddenly stung him. He was beginning to care for Jennifer Reid. She was no longer a boyhood infatuation, but a flesh-and-blood woman, more vivacious and interesting than any other woman he'd met.

He glanced at her quickly, certain she could read his thoughts, but she was gazing out the window at the fall colors mirrored in the still waters of Lake Casey.

"Will I have to be there?" she asked suddenly.

"Where?" With his daydreaming, he'd lost track of their conversation.

"At the trial for those teenage boys."

"Probably. Why?"

"There's nothing I could say." She sounded distraught. "I didn't see them."

"Ben Morgan saw them," he assured her. "He's all the witness the prosecution needs."

He turned up the hill behind the police station and took the road toward the elementary school. Classes had been dismissed hours earlier, but the playground and athletic field were crowded with cars, trucks and people.

He parked in the lot nearest the field, hopped out and opened the door for Jennifer. He lifted her out onto the packed red earth, but held onto her arm. "Can you walk okay?"

She clung to his arm, apparently unsure of her stamina. "I'll give it a try."

She had taken only a few wobbly steps when he caught a blur of red and blue out of the corner of his eye and felt its impact as Jennifer staggered against him.

"Miss Jenny! You're back!" Sissy McGinnis, carroty curls flying, denim overalls thick with red dust, clung to Jennifer's legs.

Jennifer knelt beside the girl, and Sissy threw her short, chubby arms around Jennifer's neck.

"I missed you," the little girl cried.

Millie McGinnis arrived, out of breath. "Sorry. I tried to stop her. You okay?"

Jennifer nodded and returned Sissy's hug with a fierceness Dylan envied, wishing she'd hug him like that.

"Need help putting up your booth?" Dylan, tugging his thoughts on a less dangerous heading, asked Millie.

"Gary Patterson's giving us a hand." Millie

jerked her thumb in the direction from which she'd come and blushed when she mentioned the paramedic's name.

Dylan wondered if Gary's single days were numbered.

"Tell me about your booth." Jennifer, holding Sissy's hand with one hand, stood and brushed dust from the knees of her jeans with the other.

"It's for the church sewing circle," Millie explained. "We sell handmade quilts, afghans, place mats and pot holders."

"Sandy Griffin, our dispatcher, has been crocheting like crazy all summer," Dylan said. "The ladies should make a tidy sum at the festival."

"We'll donate it to the County Rescue Squad for new equipment," Millie said.

"I could use a quilt," Jennifer said. "I'll be sure to stop by during the festival—if I can get away from the apple butter long enough."

Millie turned and gazed behind her. "I should see if Gary needs my help. C'mon, Sissy."

"I'll see you tomorrow at day care," Jennifer promised the girl.

Dylan could tell from her voice that Jennifer was tiring. He scrounged up an empty apple crate, turned it upside down and offered her a seat. From their vantage point, he identified the various booths and attractions that would be featured in the festival.

While they sat, several townsfolk approached to wish Jennifer well, including Raylene and Grover from the café, Ben Morgan and his teenaged daughter Megan and Pastor Falls from the Baptist church.

Jennifer glowed beneath their warm attention, and Dylan couldn't help marveling at the effect she had on people.

Folks in Casey's Cove were friendly enough, he knew, but they tended to keep their distance from outsiders. Dylan recalled families who'd moved to the cove over ten years ago whom the townsfolk treated politely but as if they were still strangers. But Jennifer with her effervescent personality, and now her notoriety in surviving what could have been a fatal accident, had won everybody's heart.

Including his own.

TWO DAYS LATER, as he cruised through town on his Thursday shift, Dylan was still marveling at how enthusiastically Jennifer had been accepted by his town. With such a reception, maybe she'd like Casey's Cove well enough to remain permanently, in spite of her acclaimed wanderlust.

The direction of his thoughts stunned him. If he wasn't careful, his single days, like Gary Patterson's, might be numbered, too. Before he'd met Jennifer, the idea of marriage would have sent him running in the opposite direction, but today he found himself smiling at the idea. Jennifer was just a friend, he assured himself, but you never knew where friendship might lead. For the first time in years, he was whistling as he made his rounds.

"Car Three?"

At the dispatcher's call, he jerked his thoughts back to his work and keyed the mike on his radio. "Ten-four."

"George Spivey just called. Needs you to stop by the salvage yard."

"Emergency?"

"No, but he says it's important that he speak to you ASAP."

"I'm on my way."

Dylan turned the patrol car toward the main road and paralleled the lake for a few miles before turning into Spivey's salvage yard.

George's battered tow truck sat out front, and when Dylan pulled up, George, wiping oily hands on a rag, came out of his office.

"You got a problem, Officer Blackburn."

Dylan stepped out of the car and walked to meet him. "What kind of problem?"

George twitched his head toward the garage behind him. "I pulled in Miss Bessie's Mercedes this afternoon."

"And?" Getting information out of the close-mouthed Spivey was like pulling teeth.

"It's not what you thought," George said. "Better take a look."

With a feeling of impending trouble, Dylan followed George into the garage.

Chapter Five

Jennifer stared into the bathroom mirror and applied fade cream to the persistent freckles across the bridge of her nose. The welt on her head was receding and was easily concealed by pulling her blond curls into bangs. The dark bruise on her jaw had yellowed and was well hidden by a light application of makeup.

But the damage to her heart couldn't be so easily repaired.

"You're really into this up to your neck," she scolded her scowling image. "You're falling in love. And with a policeman, for Pete's sake! Have you lost your mind?"

Her reflection didn't answer.

Jennifer rubbed harder at her freckles. "And besides being a lawman, he *hates* liars. What will you do when he finds out the whoppers you've told?"

She washed the cream off her hands and tugged at her bangs with a comb in a effort to hide the welt on her forehead. "Do you do the smart thing and avoid the man?" She shook the comb at the mirror. "Oh, no! You agree to go to the Apple Festival dance with him tonight!"

Her image smiled back at her like a lovestruck teenager.

"You're *cow-eyed*, joining the herd, just like Raylene said! Next thing you know, Grover will be adding your name to the pool at the café and taking wagers."

She flung down the comb, hurried into the bedroom, and tugged on her tennis shoes. She was due to pick up Miss Bessie in a few minutes. Her employer had been firm about not missing the opening of the festival.

Before Jennifer was halfway up the mountain, she'd decided to tell Dylan she'd changed her mind about going to the dance. She couldn't spend much more time with him without giving herself away, and coming clean with anyone, much less a policeman, was just too dangerous.

At the mansion, Miss Bessie climbed into the rental car the insurance adjustor had provided, while Jennifer and Estelle loaded boxes filled with jars of apple butter into the trunk and back seat.

"It's going to be a beautiful day," Miss Bessie said when Jennifer climbed into the driver's seat.

Jennifer peered through the windshield at the thick early-morning mist that limited her vision to a few feet in front of her. "How can you tell?"

Miss Bessie laughed. "I watch the Weather Channel. Besides, in as many of my ninety-five years as I can remember, we've never had bad weather for the opening of the festival. You wait. By ten o'clock, the mist will lift and there won't be a cloud in the sky."

Jennifer inched the car through the thick haze and scowled at the lack of visibility. "At this rate, it'll be ten o'clock before we get there."

"Just as well you're going slow," Miss Bessie said contentedly. "Wouldn't want to break any of my jars of apple butter."

As they descended the mountain, the mist remained above them, graying the morning sky. At seven forty-five when they reached the elementary school, the field was already jammed with people. Teenagers from the high school were operating a parking concession on a lower field, and hordes of tourists were ascending to the festival area.

Dylan Blackburn was directing traffic.

Jennifer took a deep breath to stop her heart from racing at the sight of him. His broad shoulders enticingly filled the dark green windbreaker of his uniform. His police cap set at a jaunty angle, he looked more handsome than ever, radiating competence and authority with every move.

He motioned Jennifer to a stop, and she rolled down her window. Along with the clean, brisk mountain air, she caught a whiff of leather, sunshine and his distinctive cologne, a provocative scent that sent her pulses racing and almost made her forget her earlier resolution to avoid the good-looking officer.

"Good morning, Miss Bessie, Jennifer." He tipped his fingertips to the brim of his hat and leaned into the window. He looked so cheerful, so pleasant, so absolutely delicious, the nearness of him made her dizzy. How was she going to tell this paragon of a man she wasn't going to the dance with him?

"Morning," she managed to mumble, her senses overwhelmed.

"You can park the car behind your booth for unloading," he said. "Visitors have to park in the lower lot."

"Thank you, Dylan," Miss Bessie said. "I'll save a jar of apple butter for you."

He straightened with a killer smile and motioned the car forward.

Grateful to get away, Jennifer accidentally gunned the motor, spinning her tires and throwing gravel in her wake. She glanced in the rearview mirror. Dylan stood with his hands on his hips, watching her.

He probably thinks I'm an idiot who doesn't know how to drive, she muttered to herself. *After all, I did manage to pitch my last car off a mountain.*

"Why should I care what he thinks of me?" she grumbled aloud.

"Why, indeed," Miss Bessie agreed with a twinkle in her eyes. "He's only the best catch in the whole county."

"I'm not fishing," Jennifer insisted, making an effort to smile.

"Sometimes the best things come along when we're not looking for them," Miss Bessie said cryptically.

"Like being pushed off a cliff?" She immediately regretted her sarcasm. Miss Bessie was a dear, sweet lady who had no idea why Jennifer had to evade Dylan Blackburn. "Sorry. You're right. Working for you has certainly turned out to be serendipitous."

"And I'm lucky to have you, my dear."

Jennifer parked the car behind the booth and began unloading boxes. As soon as Miss Bessie had unpacked the first batch of apple butter and stacked it on the counter, a crowd gathered and a line formed.

For Jennifer, the rest of the morning passed in a blur of selling apple butter and making change. Shortly before noon, Estelle arrived with another carload of the popular condiment. As soon as it was unpacked, the housekeeper drove Miss Bessie home for lunch and a much-needed nap. Estelle offered to return and bring Jennifer's lunch, but Jennifer declined.

"I'll be fine. Plenty of booths are selling food I'd like to sample. Just see that Miss Bessie gets a good rest."

Estelle's car pulled away, and Jennifer noticed with surprise that Miss Bessie's weather prediction had come true. The gray clouds had dissipated, and the clear sky was a heavenly Carolina blue.

"Hungry?" a familiar voice sounded at her elbow.

She turned to find Dylan standing beside her, holding a large basket covered with a red-checkered napkin.

"I thought you were on duty." How could she avoid the attractive officer if he kept popping up every time she turned around?

"Even a cop has to eat." He hefted the basket with a grin that made her legs feel as if they were made of Miss Bessie's apple butter. "I've brought Grover's barbecue sandwiches, Erica Gunther's apple strudel and Sally Houston's peach iced tea."

"Thanks," she said weakly.

She couldn't send him away, not when he'd been so thoughtful. Besides, the mountain air had made her ravenous, and the odors wafting from his basket made her taste buds tingle.

He turned a couple of apple crates into a table, upended two bushel baskets for seats and spread out the feast.

"Busy morning?" he asked.

She nodded, glad for an impersonal topic. "People have come from South Carolina, Georgia, Tennessee and Virginia just to buy Miss Bessie's apple butter."

"That's good for the day-care center." He unwrapped a sandwich and handed it to her. "Except for a small federal grant, Miss Bessie pays all the expenses, and a good portion comes from her apple-butter profits."

"Hey, Dylan." A couple of young women paused at the booth and cast hopeful smiles at the officer. The tweak of jealousy Jennifer felt at their attention startled her. Dylan wasn't hers, not by a long shot. The best thing that could happen would be for some local girl to lead him down the matrimonial path and out of her life.

Then why does that thought make you sad? an inner voice taunted her.

Dylan returned the girls' greetings casually, then focused his attention on his lunch. "Our traffic counter at Bottleneck Curve shows over four thousand people have come into town just this morning. There'll be thousands more before the weekend's over."

"With all those visitors, doesn't the department

need you to work tonight?'' She hoped he'd say yes. Then she wouldn't be the one to break their date.

He shook his head. "Jackson County reserve deputies fill in for the festival. Gives us locals a chance to enjoy the fun." His dark brown eyes held hers in a heated gaze. "And I'm really looking forward to the dance this evening."

"Hmmm," she answered noncommittally and glanced away.

"What's the matter?" He reached across the crate and lifted her chin with his index finger until their eyes met. "You getting cold feet?"

She grabbed at the first excuse she could think of. "Not cold feet. Just inexperienced ones. I don't know how to square dance."

He sighed with relief. "That's easy enough. I'll teach you."

"But—"

He wrinkled his brow, looking incredibly appealing even when perplexed. "Don't you want to go?"

Now was her chance. All she had to do was back out, and she'd be home free, unencumbered by more close contact with the delectable but dangerous law officer. Then she caught the shadow of disappointment that flickered across his face, a reflection of her own reluctance. She *wanted* to go to the dance with him, even though every ounce of common sense told her it was a stupid thing to do.

"Sure, I want to go." Her rebellious lips formed the exact opposite reply from what she'd intended. "I just don't want to raise your expectations about my dancing."

He leaned across again and wiped a smudge of barbecue sauce from her bottom lip with his finger, and his touch sent shivers of delight down her spine. "I didn't ask you for your dancing ability. I asked you because I like your company."

She groaned inwardly. If the man kept saying things like that, she'd never be able to stay away from him.

As if in answer to her silent prayer, the radio pinned to his shoulder squawked.

"You're wanted in Sylva at the sheriff's office," the dispatcher's voice announced. "Forensics has that report you ordered."

He keyed his mike and responded, then pushed to his feet. "Guess I'll have to take the rest of my lunch with me. Shall I pick you up tonight?"

"Sure."

Coward, she scolded herself silently, *it's still not too late to say no.*

"Eight o'clock, then," he said.

He stuffed the uneaten portion of his lunch into the basket and disappeared into the crowd. Even if she'd found the backbone to refuse him, he'd disappeared too quickly for her to cancel their date.

At least that's what she told herself.

AT EIGHT O'CLOCK, she was still having second thoughts. Her only hope for the evening was that Tommy Bennett's band would play so loudly that conversation would be impossible. If Dylan couldn't hear her, she wouldn't have to worry about telling more whoppers or giving herself away.

Dylan's knock at the front door indicated her options had run out—unless she feigned sudden illness. But such deception would only add to the lies she'd already told. Gathering her courage and praying to get through the evening without endangering her closely guarded secrets, she answered the door.

Dylan towered above her beneath the porch light. In fitted jeans, a rust-colored sweater, denim jacket and tooled leather boots, he looked better than any man had a right to. The thought of his arms around her at the dance took her breath away.

"All set?" he asked.

Speechless, she nodded, took his proffered hand and accompanied him down the steps to his pickup. He stopped beside the vehicle, pulled her to him so that her back was against his chest, and pointed skyward. "Look at that."

She turned her gaze to the heavens and drew in a quick breath. "Holy cow!"

A black velvet canopy of sky arched above them, sprinkled with too many stars to count. High on the mountain, away from the lights of the tiny town, she could see more stars in the soft darkness than she'd ever imagined on a bright city night. Dylan wrapped his arms around her, and she was achingly aware of the contact their bodies made. A shiver of pleasure spiraled down her back.

"Cold?" When he spoke, she could feel the warmth of his breath against her hair.

She shook her head. "It's incredible. I've never seen so many stars."

As they watched, a falling star arced across the sky and disappeared behind the opposite mountain.

"Ooooh," she breathed, the way a spectator reacts at a fireworks display.

He hugged her closer. "Make a wish."

She rejected the wish that popped into her head concerning Dylan. Her intention of keeping him at arm's length had already been broken. She had to get a grip on herself and her senses. "Wishes are for children."

"Then I hope I'm always a kid, because I'll never give up wishing." Although she couldn't see his face, she could hear the smile in his voice.

"Okay," she said, breaking the spell, "I wish we could go on to the dance."

He dropped his arms and stepped away from her to open the pickup's door. She felt instantly bereft and wanted to turn back to his embrace.

He's a policeman, she reminded herself. *You can't let down your guard.*

Resolutely, she climbed into the truck, fighting the emotions that threatened to expose the facts she needed to keep hidden—if she wanted to stay alive.

She decided to try psychology on herself, anything to break the hold Dylan Blackburn had on her senses and was gaining on her heart. Making a mental list, she catalogued all his faults. He was *too* handsome, *too* polite, *too* caring. She flopped back in her seat with a sigh of frustration.

Who was she kidding? Dylan Blackburn didn't *have* any faults.

Except that he worked in law enforcement.

"You're awfully quiet tonight." His voice sounded as smooth and soothing as a hot toddy in the stillness of the cab. "Tired?"

With her pulses pounding and her body coursing with adrenaline from his closeness, she felt anything but tired. But she'd already told him so many lies, what harm was one more tiny fib? She would use fatigue as an excuse to leave the dance early.

"Exhausted," she said. "Miss Bessie's booth was the busiest one at the festival today."

He reached over and clasped her hand. His skin felt warm and smooth with just a hint of calluses on his palm, and his grip was strong. "You'll get your second wind at the dance. The music's always energizing."

Much as she wanted to hold his hand, she pulled away. "I'm not a dancer, remember?"

He shot her a look as if he already knew all her secrets, and she made an effort not to squirm beneath his scrutiny. "That's what you keep telling me."

She forced a grin. "Wait till I've trampled on your toes a few times. That'll make a believer of you."

His probing expression turned torrid. "I look forward to it."

She was saved from a reply by their arrival at the school grounds. Like the rest of the festival, the dance was held outdoors. Volunteers had constructed a wooden platform and hung strings of Japanese lanterns across it. On a raised dais at one end, Tommy Bennett and the Mountaineers had already begun their performance, and couples of all ages, from children to the elderly, crowded the dance floor.

Sissy McGinnis danced with Grover, her stocking feet planted firmly atop his highly polished shoes. Ben Morgan held Miss Bessie as regally as a queen and Millie McGinnis and Gary Patterson, clenched in a tight embrace, were oblivious to all around them.

Dylan held Jennifer's arm and steered her through the crowd. As they reached the floor, the band ended one set and started another. A waltz.

With a molten look that melted her objections, Dylan pulled her onto the floor and into his arms. Her mind kept compelling her to excuse herself and sit this one out, but her heart encouraged her to snuggle deeper into his embrace, to enjoy the pressure of his hand at her waist, the warmth of his cheek against her hair and her own tingling response to the provocative masculine scent of him.

The music flowed around them, slow and dreamy, and she forgot everything and everyone, as if only the two of them danced beneath the stars in the shadow of the mountain. Entranced, she laid her head against his shoulder.

"Not yet," he murmured in her ear.

"What?" She tried to pull herself from the reverie, but the spell was too strong.

"You haven't stepped on my toes yet," he whispered in her ear. "Not once. You know what I think?"

She tipped back her head and gazed into the smoky brown depths of his eyes.

"I think, Ms. Jennifer Reid," he said with a glimmer in his eyes, "that you're a liar."

The word stung like a bucket of ice water, breaking the spell the music had woven. She stumbled—and tromped firmly on his foot.

"Whoops," he said with a grin, "I spoke too soon."

The music ended, and the crowd applauded, giving Jennifer a chance to collect her scattered thoughts. Dylan steered her off the floor to the refreshment table and handed her a cup of icy apple cider. "We need to talk."

The gravity of his expression and the resolute set of his jaw indicated he didn't mean casual chitchat. For the moment, he'd stopped being Dylan and had reverted to Officer Blackburn. Her stomach flip-flopped at the possible topics he might broach—all bad.

To hide her concern, she tried to make light of his request. "Sounds serious."

"It is."

Fear made her short of breath. Had he uncovered her past? And if he had, would he arrest her? She stumbled again as she followed him away from the crowded dance floor to a rustic bench beneath a large sugar maple. He brushed scarlet leaves from the seat, and she sank onto it quickly, afraid her quaking limbs would no longer hold her.

"What is it?" She couldn't stand the suspense any longer.

He propped one boot on the bench and folded his arms across his knee. "Remember this morning when I got that call from the forensics office in Sylva?"

She nodded, confused at the direction he'd taken.

She'd expected accusations and confrontation. She breathed easier now that they weren't forthcoming.

"Think back," he said, "to your accident. Did you see anyone on the road that night?"

His conversational shift from the forensics report to the accident bewildered her even more. "I've already told you. The headlights blinded me. I couldn't see anyone."

"Damn." He turned and sat beside her. "Ben Morgan wasn't any help either. I was hoping you would be."

"What are you talking about?"

"Those boys from the university didn't run you off the road."

"What?"

"George Spivey—he's the salvager who pulled Miss Bessie's car out of the ravine—called me yesterday. When I stopped by his garage, he showed me the left front panel of the Mercedes, or what was left of it. Clear as day on the beige exterior were streaks of black paint."

"Black?" Panic squeezed her lungs, and once again she found breathing difficult.

He nodded. "The black paint backs up what the college boys were telling us. Their two trucks are red and burgundy. No black on them anywhere. *They* didn't push you off the road. It was a different car or truck. It left its paint on the Mercedes where it hit you."

She felt dizzy with fear. Raylene's mysterious stranger had been driving a black SUV. *He* could have been the one who had forced her car off the cliff. And if he had hung around long enough afterwards, he'd known that she'd survived.

And he knew where she was.

Jennifer fought down the impulse to stand and run. She had to leave Casey's Cove as soon as possible, but without drawing attention to herself. Gazing past Dylan, she scanned the couples on the dance floor and the surrounding crowd, but saw no one who resembled the big, tough man Raylene had described.

"I'm really sorry I'm not more help." She was finally able to force words through lips wooden with fear.

"Sorry to mix business with pleasure." He stood and held out his hand. "That's not why we're here. Want to trample my feet some more?"

Even in her frightened state, she couldn't help responding to his congenial smile. She took his hand and let him lead her back onto the dance floor.

"You're a brave man, Officer Blackburn," she teased.

He pulled her closer. "If this is hazardous duty, I should request it more often."

The band was playing another slow tune, but she couldn't lose herself in the romance of the music or the deliciousness of Dylan's embrace this time. All she could think of was escape from Casey's Cove.

The sooner, the better.

With the perception she had noted the first time she met him, Dylan homed in on her change of mood. "You feeling all right?"

"My busy week is catching up with me. I'm really tired." She no longer minded telling another lie. After tonight, she'd never see him again. "Maybe I'd better leave now."

She refused to look him in the eyes, but she could feel his probing gaze. Whether he believed her no longer mattered. Her greatest concern now was running for her life.

Again.

"I'll take you home."

His tone was neutral, and she couldn't tell if she'd offended him. As hard as she tried to convince herself that his opinion of her didn't matter, she couldn't help wondering if he would miss her when she was gone.

Their walk to his truck was silent, except for the buzz of the crowd and the vibration of the Mountaineers' music on the night air. She slid onto the front seat without looking at him, and the drive back to the guest house was uninterrupted with talk. She hoped he found the silence companionable because, for the life of her, she couldn't think of anything to say. She felt more awkward than she had on her first date as a teenager.

But not less scared.

With a killer in a black SUV stalking her, she'd never been more frightened in her life.

When they arrived at her house, Dylan displayed his usual good manners. He opened the truck door for her and escorted her up the porch steps to the front door.

"I had a wonderful time." She cringed inwardly at the cliché, but her mind, numbed by fear, couldn't produce an original comment. All she could think of was getting inside, packing her belongings and planning her escape. "Thanks for inviting me."

She reached to open the door, but he pulled her hand from the knob and turned her toward him. With a gentle lift of his fingers, he tilted her chin until she faced him.

Compassion—and something hotter—glowed in his mahogany-brown eyes.

"If you need me," he said, so softly she strained to hear, "you know where to find me."

Tears welled in her eyes. Dylan was the best thing that had happened to her in the last five terrifying months. No, in the last several years. But after tonight, she would close this chapter in her life and never see him again. She railed inwardly against the unfairness.

Before she could react to his advance, Dylan pulled her into his arms and dropped his lips to hers. Abandoning herself to the poignance of a last goodbye, she returned his kiss with a fervor that temporarily drove all other thoughts from her mind. She felt *safe* in his arms, protected and cherished, and she didn't wanted to leave his embrace.

When he lifted his head, his dark eyes glowed with questions. Questions she couldn't answer. She traced her fingers along the rugged line of his jaw, etching him onto her memory. After tonight, memories were all she would have.

"Goodbye, Dylan," she whispered.

He arched his eyebrows at her choice of farewell. "I'll see you tomorrow?"

"Sure," she lied. "At the festival."

He searched her face once more, as if looking for the truth. With a grieving heart, she turned away to slip inside.

"Goodnight," she heard him whisper as she closed and locked the door.

THE FIRST HINT of dawn lightened the eastern sky when Jennifer slipped from Miss Bessie's guest house and trudged toward town. Her instinct had been to leave immediately the night before, but she knew she'd have little chance of catching a ride at midnight.

Her backpack, slung over her shoulder, held all her belongings. If she was lucky, she could sneak out of town without being seen by Dylan, and, more importantly, the mysterious stranger who stalked her.

The beauty and serenity of the surrounding mountains, as well as memories of the friends she had made in Casey's Cove, filled her with regret. She had hoped to make a home here, not slink away like a thief in the night, never to return.

After an invigorating hike in the brisk air, she reached the café. Raylene was unlocking the front door, opening for business.

"Coffee?" the waitress asked.

Jennifer slipped into her usual booth. "Hot and unleaded, please. I'll need it to keep me awake. I didn't sleep well last night."

Raylene returned with a filled mug. Jennifer was the only customer at such an early hour, and the waitress slid into the booth across from her. She eyed

Jennifer's backpack with a knowing look. "Going somewhere?"

Jennifer sipped her coffee and nodded. "The airport. Know anybody who can give me a lift?"

"So you saw him, too?"

"Him?"

Raylene checked her reflection in the front window and patted a wayward strand of teased hair into place. "The guy in the SUV who has the picture that looks like you. I saw him this morning on my way into work."

Almost dropping her coffee cup in surprise, Jennifer peered out the window in alarm. The streets of the cove remained deserted in the early hours of Saturday morning. No signs of a black sport utility vehicle. "Where was he?"

"Parked at Bottleneck Curve."

Jennifer sank low on the bench. "If he stays there, he can see everyone who enters and leaves town." In desperation, she leaned across the table and grabbed the waitress's hands. "Can you think of anyone who can drive me to the airport? Smuggle me past him?"

Raylene thought for a second. "What about Dylan?"

Jennifer shook her head. "Out of the question."

With narrowed eyes, the waitress studied her. "You *are* in trouble, aren't you, hon?"

Jennifer avoided her gaze. "Sorry, but I can't tell you about it. Believe me, though, I haven't broken any laws." She hesitated. "At least not any major ones."

"Then why not ask Dylan for help?"

Jennifer shrugged. "It's too complicated to explain."

"What about Miss Bessie?"

"She can't see well enough to drive. I left her a note at the guest house saying I was called away suddenly on a family emergency."

Raylene grimaced. "Honey, you don't *have* any family. You told me so yourself."

Jennifer forced an apologetic smile. "I told you it's complicated. But I have to leave town. It could be a matter of life and death."

Raylene's kindly face twisted into a frown. "With the festival in full swing, I don't know anybody who can drive you to the airport today."

"Is there a limo I could call?"

Raylene nodded. "Sure, but don't you think the guy who's looking for you will check out a limo headed for the airport?"

Thinking hard, Jennifer buried her head in her hands. When an idea struck her, she lifted her hopeful gaze to Raylene. "Is there any way out of the cove that doesn't go past Bottleneck Curve?"

"Not by road. There's lots of footpaths over the mountains, but—" Raylene stopped short and snapped her fingers. Her aging eyes brightened. "I have an idea."

Jennifer's dashed hopes soared. "A way out?"

"Not exactly, but it might work. Give me your breakfast order so Grover can get started on it. You're going to need all the energy you can get."

HOURS LATER, Jennifer kicked her way through drifts of fallen leaves that clogged the forest trail and crested the top of a ridge. Winded from the steep climb, she settled on a large boulder to rest her aching feet and catch her breath. Over three miles below, Casey's Cove nestled like a miniature village at the lake's edge. Mountains stretched around her in every direction. On a peak across the valley, Miss Bessie's Victorian mansion glowed white in the sunlight.

Glancing up the spine of the ridge about a hundred yards ahead, Jennifer spotted Raylene's family's hunting cabin among a stand of evergreens, just where the kind-hearted waitress had told her it would be.

After her breathing had eased, Jennifer climbed toward the rustic log cabin, accessible only by the winding, rugged foot trail that began at the back of Raylene's café. The waitress had suggested Jennifer remain in the cabin until her stalker quit town. Meanwhile, Raylene would spread the word that Jennifer had left for the airport that morning. Once the stranger had disappeared and the festival ended, Raylene promised to drive Jennifer to the Asheville airport herself.

Jennifer had begged Raylene not to tell Miss Bessie, Dylan or anyone else where she was hiding. She would be safer from the stalker if everyone assumed she'd left town.

She mounted the steps of the porch, fumbled with the key Raylene had given her and opened the door. Sunlight streamed through the windows, catching hundreds of dust motes dancing in the air. The one-room building was primitive. No electricity, no running water, but there were lanterns, an outhouse and a nearby spring. She would look on her crude accommodations as an adventure.

Jennifer slung her backpack on the table and unpacked the lunch Grover had prepared for her. The long hike up the mountain had made her ravenous, but the café cook's hearty sandwich stuck in her throat, blocked by the lump that held back her tears. She was tired of running, tired of looking over her shoulder, tired of being afraid for her life, but she didn't know any way she could change things.

If she stopped running, she'd die.

She gave up trying to eat and removed a blanket from the cedar chest at the foot of the bed. She hadn't slept at all the night before, and now she curled on top of the bare mattress, willed her aching muscles to relax, shut her eyes to the demons that pursued her and went to sleep.

Shivering in the cold, she awoke hours later at dusk. After gathering wood from the supply piled beneath the shelter of the porch roof, she built a fire in the stone fireplace and picked at the provisions Raylene had provided. At the rate she wasn't eating, her supplies would last a week.

The sun sank quickly behind the western ridges, leaving bone-chilling cold and inky darkness in its wake. The quiet and isolation made Jennifer jumpy. She secured the cabin door and windows, pulled the dusty curtains and settled on the musty, overstuffed sofa to wait for dawn. After her long afternoon nap, she doubted she could sleep anymore and wished she'd brought a book to keep her company.

She passed the time contemplating possible hiding places and where she might run once the weekend had ended.

The sudden snap of a twig on the path outside brought her to her feet. Peering between the curtains, she spotted a dark silhouette approaching the cabin on the trail that climbed the ridgeline.

It was a man.

A *big* man.

Terrified that the stalker had somehow discovered her location, she searched the cabin frantically for a weapon. The only protection she found was a large iron skillet, so heavy she had to heft it with two hands.

"Hello! Anybody there?" His cry broke the stillness.

Not recognizing the deep voice, Jennifer didn't answer. She sat absolutely still, listening to the too-loud sound of her own breathing and praying he would think the cabin deserted and go away. With a glance at the glow of the fire and the realization the stranger could see smoke curling from the chimney, her hopes vanished.

"Hello?" the raspy voice called again.

Jennifer crouched beside the front door, the cabin's only entrance or exit and hefted the frying pan.

Footsteps sounded on the front porch, and the man's tread shook the floorboards beneath her feet. Her breath caught in her throat. Unless she took him by surprise, she didn't have a chance. Even if he didn't have a gun, he more than outweighed her in a hand-to-hand fight.

Silently, she cursed the fact that she'd never learned karate.

The doorknob rattled.

The door shook, but it didn't open.

She waited, hoping for the sound of retreating footsteps, praying the man would believe her gone and go away.

With a suddenness that made her jump, the door's locking mechanism rattled and clicked. Her heartbeats thundered in her ears, and she bit back a moan of dismay.

He was picking the lock.

Struggling against the impulse to faint, she lifted the iron skillet high over her head and waited as the door swung open.

Chapter Six

Jennifer held her breath and gripped the handle of the skillet until her joints ached and her knuckles whitened. The enormous man stepped across the threshold into the dim light of the room, and she brought the pan down hard.

With the lightning reflexes of a cat, he ducked and rolled. The descending skillet encountered only air, jerking her off balance and dragging her almost to the floor. She staggered and barely managed to remain upright.

The intruder landed on his feet in front of the fireplace, turned and faced her.

With a startled cry, she dropped the skillet on her foot.

He wasn't Raylene's mysterious stranger.

He was Dylan Blackburn.

"At least my reaction time has improved since our first meeting." His expression was somber, and he rubbed the bridge of his nose, as if remembering that encounter.

"You scared the living daylights out of me!"

Angry now that her fear had fled, she hobbled to

the sofa and plopped onto the cushions, raising a small cloud of dust when her behind hit the seat.

He was unrepentant. "I called out. You didn't answer."

"I didn't recognize your voice," she said accusingly. "You sound different."

"Allergies. I had to tromp through acres of goldenrod and ragweed to reach you." He pulled a large handkerchief from his pocket, buried his face in it and sneezed.

"How did you know I was here?" She yanked off her sneaker and sock and rubbed gingerly at the expanding black-and-blue mark where the skillet had bounced off her foot.

"Raylene told me."

Jennifer tasted the bitterness of betrayal. "She promised she wouldn't."

His face settled into hard lines, as formidable and unmoving as the ancient mountain beneath them. "*Raylene* knows better than to lie to me."

She sensed the challenge in his statement and became immediately defensive. "What are you saying?"

Shrugging out of his down-filled parka, he settled on the sofa beside her. Before she could protest, he reached for her bare foot and gently kneaded it with his large, gentle hands. If she hadn't felt so wary, she might have moaned with pleasure.

"You should be more careful," he lectured.

"And you should have identified yourself," she snapped, glad the subject had changed.

Without ceasing his massage, he scrutinized her face. "Have *you* lied to me?"

She turned to stare at the flickering flames in the stone fireplace to avoid his penetrating look. Struggling to think of an answer that wouldn't dig her into deeper trouble, she countered with a question of her own. "What did Raylene tell you?"

"Only that you were staying up here for the weekend. I checked with her after Miss Bessie called to say you'd left. Not only is Miss Bessie genuinely worried about you, she'd been counting on you to help with the festival." Disapproval edged his voice and etched a frown on his face.

Fighting off spasms of guilty conscience, Jennifer sank deeper into the sofa. She focused on her foot, dwarfed by his hands, unable to face him, not knowing what to say.

"I hope," he said in a challenging tone, "you wouldn't disappoint Miss Bessie without a damn good reason. Want to tell me what it is?"

Jennifer withdrew her foot from his grasp and curled into the farthest corner of the sofa. "I don't know where to start."

He rose, placed a log on the fire, and stirred life into the flames. "Why did you leave Casey's Cove?"

Lifting her head, she glared at him, standing with his back to the fire, his face deep in shadow, his eyes shuttered by half-closed lids. "Someone's trying to kill me."

She waited for him to laugh and make light of her plight, but he only nodded. "Go on."

She gulped a deep breath and plunged ahead. "A few days after I arrived, a stranger approached Raylene. He had a picture she said looked like me. He said I was a long-lost relative he was trying to locate. Raylene was suspicious. She didn't like his looks, so she told him she hadn't seen me."

"What makes you believe he meant to harm you?"

She wished Dylan would stop being the consummate lawman and return to being her friend. A friend would be much easier to talk to than the austere man before her. "He was driving a black sport utility vehicle."

Dylan settled onto the other end of the sofa. "Like the one that forced you off the mountain last weekend."

It wasn't a question. He'd made the connection immediately.

She nodded. "Raylene said he showed up again this morning at Bottleneck Curve, watching everyone who comes and goes from the cove."

"Any idea who he is?"

"No, but I know who sent him."

He waited, obviously well-trained in interview techniques. Under different circumstances, she would have counted on his friendship and leaned on him for support. And she would have welcomed his professional assistance. But she had offended him as both a friend and a professional with her lies, lies he was yet unaware of.

"It's a long story." She stalled, hoping to delay her confession as long as possible. Until this minute, she hadn't realized how much she valued Dylan's opinion of her, an opinion that would plummet like a brick in a pond once he knew the whole truth.

"We've got all night. I'm not going anywhere." His deep, rich voice, husky with allergies, resounded through the confines of the small room.

He shoved to his feet, crossed to a set of cabinets on the opposite wall and removed a coffeepot and tin of coffee. He filled the pot from a bucket she'd brought from the spring behind the cabin, added grounds, and hung it by its wire handle from a hook above the fire.

"You've been here before," she observed.

"Raylene's family has let me use this place since I was a kid."

"For hunting?"

"Most of my hunting I did with a camera. I don't like killing."

She shivered at his expression. He didn't like killing. Or liars or cheats or lawbreakers. He wasn't going to like her very much either when he had all the facts.

He gathered mugs, powdered creamer and sugar from the cabinet and arranged them on the low table in front of the fire. "Have you eaten?"

"Raylene packed sandwiches for me. Want one?" She started to rise.

He pushed her back with a firm but gentle hand. "Stay off that foot. I'll find them."

He located the food, selected a sandwich and sat cross-legged on the floor before the low table. She watched him eat, fascinated by the paradox of his rugged appetite and good manners. The coffee perked above the fire, filling the room with its aroma. He handed her half a sandwich, and she nibbled it, surprised to discover she was hungry after all.

Had the occasion been different, she would have found the atmosphere romantic: a handsome man, the rugged planes of his face softly lit by the glow of the fire, his proximity both stimulating and comforting; the wind howling eerily around the log corners of the cabin while they sat snugly inside, shielded from the bleak darkness of the chilly night; an intimate meal, shared by two people obviously attracted to one another.

But Officer Dylan Blackburn was all business, determined to discover why she'd deserted Miss Bessie and fled town, and the atmosphere was tense.

He removed the pot from its hook, filled the mugs and handed her one. Instead of returning to the floor or the opposite end of the sofa, he pulled an overstuffed chair beside her, sat facing her and sipped his coffee. "Whenever you're ready."

Delaying, she emptied half her mug before she finally spoke. "I didn't *exactly* lie to you."

His generous mouth quirked in an ironic half grin. "A half truth is still a lie. It's kind of like being a little pregnant."

Chastised, she nodded. He obviously wasn't going to make this easy for her. "I omitted a previous employment from my job resume."

More disapproval flitted through the depths of his eyes, glittering golden brown in the firelight. "Before or after Nashville?"

"Before. I worked six months as a legal secretary for an attorney in Atlanta until the end of May."

The intriguing lines of his face settled deeper into a frown, and she suppressed the desire to lean forward and erase it with the tips of her fingers. She sighed. His censure would grow as her story unfolded.

"You said you had no skills or training," he said flatly.

Another lie she'd told him, but on the Richter scale of her many falsehoods, less than a one-point-zero. "I took a few courses at night."

"Go on."

He seemed cold, professional, totally objective. Realizing he'd never hold her or trust her again broke her heart, but she continued. She owed him an explanation. At least as much as she could safely give him.

"The attorney I worked for, Larry Crutchfield, has his office in the Buckhead district of Atlanta. He moves in the upper echelons of Atlanta society—patron of the symphony, officer in the Chamber of Commerce, and he's also on the hospital board."

If Dylan was impressed, he didn't show it. "I assume you're going somewhere with this story?"

She nodded, swallowed more coffee to wet her dry mouth, and continued. "I liked my job, but Crutchfield was a real pain. He has an overinflated opinion of himself."

"Is that why you quit?"

She shook her head. "One Friday night in May, I realized I'd left my wallet in my desk at the office and went back to retrieve it. I let myself in with my key and was opening my desk drawer when I heard angry voices coming from Crutchfield's office. I recognized my boss's voice. It took a few seconds, but I identified the other man. It was Max Thorne, the firm's biggest corporate client.''

Inundated by dark memories of that calamitous evening, she began to shake. Dylan leaned forward and clasped her hands. ''You okay?''

She nodded, but gripped his fingers hard, grateful for his warmth and the security of his presence. ''Before I could sneak out, I heard two loud bangs that sounded as if they'd come from Crutchfield's private office. Then everything went quiet. I grabbed my wallet and left.''

Embarrassed by her show of fear, she released his hands and leaned back into the corner of the sofa. ''By the time I arrived home, I had convinced myself the sharp reports I'd heard had been the backfire of cars in traffic on the avenue.''

Dylan kept his eyes riveted on her face. If she lied even so much as a smidgen, he'd know it, so she kept strictly to the truth.

''I had a habit of arriving at work a half hour early so I could read the morning paper and have coffee at my desk. The next Monday, I followed my same routine, but when I opened the front section of the paper, a headline jumped out at me. Max Thorne had been found murdered the day before.''

''Where?''

''Outside Atlanta. Buried beneath a mountain of debris in a landfill, he was discovered by kids treasure-hunting among the trash. He'd been shot. Twice.''

"Did you go to the police?''

In retrospect, what she should have done seemed so simple, but she hadn't been thinking clearly at the time. "I told the other secretary in the office I wasn't feeling well and was going home. Before I left, I took the mail into Crutchfield's office to leave on his desk. I noticed immediately that his carpeting had been replaced over the weekend. I was positive then he had killed Max Thorne.''

"Circumstantial,'' Dylan muttered.

She nodded in agreement. "That's one reason I didn't go to the cops. The other was the power of Crutchfield's reputation and his army of influential friends. Who would believe me over a pillar of the Atlanta community?''

She could almost see the wheels working in Dylan's mind. "The police could have searched for his old carpet,'' he said, "and sprayed his car with Luminol for traces of blood, checked for gun ownership—''

"I was too terrified to think straight. All I wanted was to get out of Atlanta as soon as possible. I hurried home and packed my belongings. But before I could leave the house, Crutchfield was there, beating on the front door. I fled out the back, and he chased me. After I caught a bus, I was able to lose him in downtown traffic.''

Dylan sat back in his chair with a thoughtful expression. "So you think Crutchfield sent the guy in the black SUV to kill you? Isn't that a stretch?''

She shook her head. "He *knows* that I know. I've seen it on his face."

"When he came to your house?"

"When he caught sight of me through the train window in Chicago. I was running as far as I could from Atlanta. From the hatred in his eyes, I knew he hadn't followed me to deliver my severance pay."

"Have you seen him again since Chicago?"

She shook her head. "I headed out west, but realized he knew I was going in that direction, so I backtracked to Memphis. I went from there to Nashville, but I bailed out of town when I heard some man had been asking questions about me. Knowing Crutchfield, he's hired someone to make certain I never go to the police."

"If you'd gone to the police immediately, you'd have saved yourself a lot of grief." He had resumed his official demeanor, unyielding and stern.

"Maybe," she admitted, "but I'll never know for sure."

"Do you intend to keep running the rest of your life?"

She lifted her chin defiantly. It was easy for him to say what she should have done, what she ought to do. *He* didn't have a killer after him. "I thought I'd go to New York City. Disappearing should be easy among all those people."

"If Crutchfield murdered Max Thorne, he should be punished. Looks like you're the only one who can bring him to justice."

She bolted upright and winced as her injured foot hit the sofa's edge. "Don't lay a guilt trip on me!

My life means more to me than justice for Larry Crutchfield.''

Dylan couldn't have looked more disgusted if she'd admitted to cannibalism. "Without justice, society will revert to barbarism."

"There're hundreds of barbarians roaming the streets in this country. One more or less makes little difference, but my life means a hell of a lot to me."

Grim-faced, he nodded. "So, you'll be wanting a ride to the airport."

His quick acceptance of her defiance took the wind from her sails. Maybe he was that anxious to be rid of her. "If I can get past the stranger at Bottleneck Curve."

He glanced at her bruised foot. "You're not trekking out of here on that foot anytime soon. You'll have to keep your weight off that injury for a day or so."

She started to protest, but the excruciating throb in her foot stopped her.

"In the meantime—" Dylan reached for his parka and tugged it on "—I'll check out this guy and his SUV. If I can connect him to your accident, I can lock him up."

"You're going down the mountain in the dark?"

"The trail's well-marked, and I've used it since I was a kid. I'll check back in a day or two to take you to the airport." He crossed to the door and turned back toward her. His expression softened for the first time since his arrival. "Will you be all right?"

She forced a smile. "I have everything I need."

"You won't be frightened?"

His concern touched her, and she fought against the tears that welled in her eyes. "Not if you leave that skillet within reach."

With a grin, he handed her the frying pan. "Just be careful of that other foot, or you won't have a leg to hobble on."

With a cavalier wave, he stepped out the door and closed it behind him.

Listening to his footsteps descending the path, she'd never felt more lonely in her life.

TWO DAYS LATER, Dylan started up the path to Raylene's cabin before daybreak. By the time he had crested the final ridge, the sun was high and the morning mist had evaporated.

He wondered how Jennifer had fared for two days alone in the cabin. He figured she'd been safe enough with no one knowing her whereabouts. The only hitch was whether she could stand her own company for that long.

The cabin came in sight, and he caught the glimmer of sunlight on a head of blond curls. Jennifer lounged on the porch steps, eyes closed, her face tilted toward the sun. From her peaceful expression, he decided she'd come through her solitary experience just fine.

She must have heard or sensed his approach, because suddenly she leaped to her feet and ran down the path to meet him. With her golden hair tossing in the wind, her green eyes shining, her slender figure light and graceful, she was the most attractive woman he'd ever seen.

And the most aggravating.

Not that she'd broken any laws—that he knew of. But she'd misrepresented herself and lied about her past, not only to him, but to Miss Bessie. If the man who was on her trail had caught up with her, he could have harmed not only Jennifer, but those around her, including Miss Bessie and Sissy McGinnis.

The possibility made him remember....

He shoved dark memories of Johnny Whitaker's death from his mind, and returned his thoughts to Jennifer. In spite of her untruths, she was an engaging woman. She certainly had spunk and backbone. She'd managed to elude a killer for months, and she didn't shirk from protecting herself or even staying alone on a deserted mountaintop. Most women he knew were too squeamish to survive as well as she had under the circumstances. In spite of all she'd been through the past few months, she appeared to have no regrets about the past and no real anxiety about her future, as long as she stayed one step ahead of the mysterious man who stalked her.

But, he reminded himself, she was also silvertongued, able to spin tales that suited her situation, even if they bore no resemblance to the truth. How many more lies had she told him than the ones she'd admitted to?

Dylan hardened his heart toward the delectable woman. Otherwise he might find himself entirely too attracted to Jennifer Reid, a woman who packed a powerful wallop of trouble in a very pretty package.

"Your foot's better," he noted when she reached him.

She smiled, and her warmth almost melted the icy casing in which he'd secured his feelings. "It's fine—if you don't count an ugly patch of chartreuse and yellow skin."

"Then you're ready to hike out?"

She cocked her head and considered him for an instant with a piercing look. A hint of sadness flickered across her face, as if she'd sensed the barrier he'd erected between them. "I'll only need a minute to pack."

She pivoted on her heel and dashed back toward the cabin, her trim hips moving provocatively as she ran. With a sigh for all the things that might have been, Dylan shifted his gaze to the north. The high peaks of the Blue Ridge Parkway lined the horizon, and the sight of the massive, silent sentinels, immovable and unchanged during the course of his life and his father's and grandfather's before him, calmed him. He made his decision. He would drive Jennifer to the airport to catch her plane to New York City.

Then he would do what he had to do.

She returned minutes later, her backpack slung over her shoulder. Dylan turned and headed down the mountain.

"Wait," she grabbed his arm. "What about the man in the SUV? Is he gone?"

He nodded. "I'll fill you in while we walk."

"Okay." She fell in step behind him on the narrow path.

He had to call over his shoulder to speak to her.

"Your man was still at Bottleneck Curve yesterday morning. From what the night-shift officer told me, the guy must have slept in his SUV, because he hadn't moved it since yesterday."

"Did you talk to him?"

He held a low branch until she'd cleared it so it wouldn't whip her in the face. "I ran a check on his plates first. His vehicle is registered in Texas to a company called Final Choice. Ever hear of it when you were working for Crutchfield?"

"Not that I remember. Gruesome selection of words for a hit man, don't you think?"

He heard her stumble on the path behind him, but when he turned to assist her, she was plowing gamely through the drifts of fallen leaves.

Dylan slowed to cross a downed tree trunk and gave her a hand in climbing over it. "I figure it's a dummy corporation. I couldn't find anything about it on the Internet, and there were no phone listings."

"Did you ask the man about it?"

"Yeah. He said it's a company of private investigators who work throughout the country. Their specialty is finding lost relatives and friends."

"Did you believe him?" Her breath was coming in short gasps, but she didn't ask him to slow his pace.

"He had a business card. But anyone with a computer can produce those by the dozen."

He shortened his steps to ease her descent, and she almost ran into the back of him. "Maybe we should stop for a breather," he said.

"I'm fine," she insisted.

He took in her reddened cheeks and the sheen of perspiration on her forehead. "I wouldn't mind a rest," he said.

She shrugged, dropped her backpack and leaned against the nearest tree. "This guy have a name?"

Dylan settled on a moss-covered boulder. "Michael Johnson was the name on his Texas driver's license. I ran him through the crime computers, but he came up clean."

"What about his vehicle? He must have scraped it when he hit me."

Dylan shook his head. "There were no scratches or dings on the right front quarter-panel."

She became very still, almost as if she'd stopped breathing. "You think I'm lying about him, don't you?"

"Your track record in the truth department is spotty, to put it mildly."

She slumped against the tree and slid to the ground. "I knew you wouldn't believe me. I never should have told you."

She looked so delicate, so vulnerable and unhappy, he wanted to leap up and hold her, assure her he'd take care of her. At least that's what his heart was telling him. His head reminded him she was a manipulator with her concocted stories, and he'd better sort out the truth before he invested any of his emotions in her.

His head won the war within him, and he remained on the boulder. "He's had plenty of time to have the damage repaired. Besides, you didn't make up the black SUV paint on Miss Bessie's Mercedes."

She stared at her feet, refusing to meet his gaze. "No, I didn't."

"And you didn't make up the picture he had of you."

Her head snapped up. "Did you see it?"

Dylan nodded. "Guess you changed your looks when you went into hiding. I kind of like you with red hair and more freckles."

She blushed, but whether at his compliment or the fact that he'd caught her in another deception, he couldn't tell.

"Did he call me by name?" she asked.

Dylan didn't blame her for being frightened. Michael Johnson was one tough character. Dylan thought back to his conversation with the rough-looking out-of-towner. "No. When he showed me your picture, I told him you'd left Casey's Cove the day before, that your employer had driven you to the airport. He asked where you were headed."

Her eyes widened with panic. "What did you tell him?"

"That you had relatives in San Diego. Figured that's about as far as you can get from New York City within the continental U.S."

"You *lied* for me?"

He felt heat rise up his neck and flood his face. "Yeah, I guess I did."

"So you admit that sometimes lies are okay—if they're used to protect people?"

Flustered, he stood and brushed forest debris from the seat of his jeans. "I believe what goes around, comes around. That goes for lies, too."

He continued down the trail, no longer shortening his stride to accommodate her. He'd broken his own code for this woman, something he'd never done in his life. If he stayed around her much longer, she'd corrode all his values.

An hour later, after a long, silent descent, they reached the main street of Casey's Cove where Dylan had parked his truck. Jennifer hobbled behind him, and he felt a twinge of conscience when he realized her bruised foot had probably been bothering her the entire way and she'd never complained.

Panting for breath, she climbed into the truck cab without a word as he held the door open. She leaned back against the seat and closed her eyes.

"Wait here," he said. "I'll be right back."

In a few minutes he returned with a large soft drink in a paper cup and some Tylenol capsules he'd coaxed from Raylene. "These should help the pain in your foot."

Her look of gratitude almost battered down the defenses he'd constructed against her. While she washed down the capsules with soda, he climbed into the cab and started the truck.

The sooner he put her on the plane to New York, the better.

As they rounded Bottleneck Curve, Jennifer glanced around nervously. "Are you sure he's gone?"

"I followed him out of town. He took Highway 441 south out of Dillsboro. Maybe he's headed for San Diego."

When they reached the main highway, Dylan

turned east toward Asheville and the airport. Since her question, Jennifer had sat silently, but her glance alternated from every side road they passed to the rearview mirror. Apparently she wasn't convinced Michael Johnson—Dylan doubted that was the man's real name—had actually left the area. If he were in her place, he'd be just as skeptical. Maybe her cautious nature was all that had kept her alive the past few months.

Or maybe her entire story was a fabrication, and Michael Johnson was really searching for her on behalf of a relative.

Then why did he run her off the road?

If that's what actually happened. For all Dylan knew, Jennifer might have struck the SUV in an attempt to get away, then rebounded over the edge of the mountain. That was the trouble with lies. When somebody told you one, you never knew if you could trust anything else they told you.

"How was the rest of the festival?" she asked. "Did Miss Bessie sell all her apple butter?"

"She sold out on Saturday. Millie McGinnis stepped in to help after you took off." He tried, but couldn't keep the censure from his voice.

His tone must have hit home, because she slid a little lower in her seat. "I'm sorry I had to leave. I didn't know what else to do."

He started to say she should have come to him, but they'd been down that conversational road before and reached a dead end. "Megan, Ben Morgan's daughter, was crowned Apple Queen. And the sewing circle raised enough money to complete what they needed for a new ambulance for the rescue squad.''

"I'm sorry I missed everything. I was really looking forward to it."

She sounded sincere, but he'd lost his trust in anything she said.

They covered the distance to the airport in silence, Dylan lost in his thoughts, Jennifer eyeing every passing car suspiciously. When they reached the terminal, he turned into the short-term parking area.

"No need for you to get out," she said quickly. "Aren't you on duty soon?"

Dylan nodded, wondering whether her comment stemmed from concern for his schedule or eagerness to be rid of him. "I'm working the afternoon shift."

She grabbed her backpack. "Just drop me off at Departures."

He pulled the truck to the curb. "You're taking the next flight to New York?"

Adjusting the strap on her backpack, she avoided his gaze. "Don't know how soon that will be. You can go on. You don't need to wait."

"Jennifer—" Now that she was leaving, he felt at a loss for words. In spite of his conviction that she was gold-plated trouble, he couldn't shake his feelings for her. He hated thinking of her alone in the big city, even if she'd proved she could take care of herself.

She lifted her face, and her guileless expression and the hint of tears in her eyes made him feel like an ogre. He shouldn't send her off alone, but damned if he knew what else to do.

"Yes?" Her voice was only a whisper.

"Write to me when you get to New York. Let me know where you're staying."

Disappointment flitted across her face. "Sure."

Without a backward glance, she slid from the cab and hurried into the terminal, limping only slightly on her injured foot.

He watched her go with conflicting emotions, partly glad he wouldn't have to deal with her lies again, partly destitute at watching her walk out of his life forever.

Chapter Seven

Jennifer lifted her head from the microfiche viewer and rubbed her tired eyes. She had flown out of Asheville three days ago, but in many ways, it seemed like years. She gazed out the library window. Dark clouds were gathering on the southwest horizon, a sure sign of an approaching cold front, one more than likely accompanied by rain. If she wanted to reach home without getting soaked, she had to get a move on.

She scooped up copies of newspaper articles, stuffed them into her backpack, and headed for the nearest exit. If she hurried, she could catch the next bus. She bolted down the stairs and raced to the corner just as the bus approached and the first drops of rain pelted her face.

She stepped onto the bus, but strong hands grabbed her from behind and yanked her back to the sidewalk. Screeching in alarm, she swung her backpack at her attacker.

The big man ducked, then grabbed the backpack from her hands. "As least this isn't as lethal as an iron frying pan," he said.

Mouth open, she froze in surprise.

"Need me to call the cops, miss?" the bus driver called to her. He'd witnessed the entire altercation through the bus's open door.

She shook her head. "Never mind. He's a friend."

"The way you was yelling, didn't sound like no friend." With a dubious look, the driver closed the doors and put the bus into gear.

Still shaking from her scare, Jennifer stood in the cloud of diesel fumes and glared at man who'd grabbed her. "That's the *third* time you've almost scared me to death."

Dylan tossed her the backpack and grinned. "How could I scare *you* to death when *I'm* in Atlanta and *you're* supposed to be in New York City?"

Anger had replaced her fear, but it was tempered with such happiness at the sight of him, she didn't know whether to smack the smug expression off his handsome face or throw her arms around him and tell him how glad she was to see him again. Conflicted, she did neither.

"Are you following me?" she accused him.

He placed his fists on his hips and stared down at her. "If I had been following you, I'd have headed north. What are you doing in Atlanta?"

"It's a long story."

"You're full of long stories, aren't you?"

The rain had increased in intensity, and rivulets were running off her hair and into her eyes. She turned up the collar of her jacket against the deluge. "It's raining cats and dogs, and that was the last bus for the next hour."

He jerked his thumb over his shoulder, and she recognized his pickup truck parked across the street. "I'll drive you wherever you're headed. That'll give you a chance to tell me your long story."

The rain fell harder. He broke into a run for the truck, and she dashed behind him, anxious for cover from the cold downpour and piercing wind. Once inside, she pushed soggy wisps of hair from her eyes. "Why are you here?"

"I asked you first." He started the engine. "Where to?"

She gave directions to her place and leaned back against the seat. The wipers swished across the windshield in a hypnotic rhythm, the truck's heater blew comforting hot air on her wet, cold feet, and for the first time in days she felt safe again—now that her initial panic had passed.

When Dylan had grabbed her off the bus she'd been terrified and had turned, expecting to find that Larry Crutchfield's hit man finally had her in his clutches. She'd never been so glad to see Dylan, but she wouldn't tell him so. Ever since he'd learned about the lies she'd told, disapproval of her had been stamped all over him. No point in encouraging a man who apparently wanted nothing to do with her.

Then why was he in Atlanta?

"Is this it?" He had pulled the truck into a parking space along the curb in front of the ancient house where she'd rented a two-room apartment on the second floor.

"Home, sweet home." She reached for the door

handle. "Want to come up? I brew a mean cup of tea."

"I'm still waiting for your long story."

"That, too. First, I want to shuck these wet clothes."

They left the truck and raced through the raindrops to the rickety stairs that climbed the outside of the building. On the top landing, Jennifer fumbled for her key in her backpack, unlocked the door and stepped inside. Dylan followed.

She crossed to a table behind the sofa and flicked on a lamp. Its soft glow filled the room but did nothing to hide the shabbiness of her surroundings. She hadn't noticed before how faded and worn everything looked, but seeing it through Dylan's eyes, she winced. At least it was clean.

"This is only temporary," she said.

He shook rain from his jacket, hung it on a hook by the door and turned to her with a perceptive smile, but not before she'd glimpsed the revolver tucked in his belt at the small of his back. For the first time since his unexpected arrival, she remembered that he was a policeman and that she still had secrets to hide.

"I'm sure all will be explained in your long story," he said.

"You want a towel?"

"No, thanks. Only my jacket got wet."

"Make yourself comfortable. I'll be back in a minute."

In the bathroom, she removed her wet clothes, tugged on dry jeans and a sweatshirt and grimaced at herself in the mirror. With her hair hanging in wet, lank strands, she looked and felt like a drowned rat.

Why should you care what you look like? she asked herself. *You blew your chances with Mr. Law-and-Order days ago.*

With a sigh of resignation, she pulled a comb through her damp curls and went into the kitchen. In a few minutes, she had prepared a tray with a pot of spiced tea and a plate of bakery muffins, warmed in the microwave.

Stiffening her spine for the upcoming interrogation, she swept into the living room and forced herself to smile. "Better get it while it's hot."

Dylan turned from gazing out the front window, took the tray and placed it on the coffee table. She perched on the sofa, filled a mug and handed it to him, avoiding his scrutinizing stare, a look that made the hairs on the back of her neck stand erect. He was a hard man to keep secrets from.

"Your long story?" he prodded.

She drew a deep breath. "When you left me at the Asheville airport, I had every intention of flying to New York."

"So you said," he noted skeptically.

"The airlines couldn't book me a flight straight through to New York for over six hours—so I decided to backtrack and come through Atlanta."

Dylan nodded. "We have a saying in our part of the country. If you die and go to Hell, you still have to layover in Atlanta first."

Her hopes rose at his touch of humor. Maybe he hadn't written her off entirely after all. "In spite of the longer distance, that route meant I'd arrive in New York sooner and pay less for my ticket,'' she explained.

"So," he said, "you're still here. Miss your connecting flight?''

She shook her head. ''On the trip from Asheville, I kept thinking about Miss Bessie and how I'd let her down. I'd give anything if I could go back to Casey's Cove and make things up to her.''

He nodded, eyeing her warily as if unsure whether to believe her. ''Your return would mean a lot to Miss Bessie. And to a lot of the folks in town who befriended you.''

She hadn't lied about Miss Bessie. The eccentric but affectionate old woman had been the closest thing to family she'd experienced in years. Jennifer felt genuinely sorry for deserting her during the festival.

What Jennifer neglected to mention was her reluctance to leave Dylan as part of her motive for returning to Atlanta. Because he so obviously disapproved of her, she wanted to do something to reinstate herself in his good graces, and she'd realized she couldn't do that by running away.

''I can't go back to Casey's Cove until it's safe, and it won't be safe until Larry Crutchfield is behind bars.''

The wariness in his expression dissolved, replaced by what appeared to be grudging approval. ''You said a few days ago you were too scared for your life to return here.''

She lifted her face and met his gaze squarely. ''I

am scared. But if Crutchfield isn't caught, I'll be scared the rest of my days. That's no way to live.''

''So you've decided to give up life on the run?''

Encouraged, she continued. ''I've decided to stay in Atlanta to see what evidence I can dig up that points to Crutchfield. That's what I was doing in the library this afternoon, researching every news article I could find about Max Thorne's murder.''

She stopped and sipped her tea. Dylan continued to stare at her, but his expression had turned guarded, as if hiding his feelings.

''Now,'' she said, ''it's your turn. Why are *you* in Atlanta? And how did you find me?''

''I wasn't looking for you.''

She experienced a painful twinge of rejection. ''It's an awfully big city to run into someone by accident.''

Dylan turned to the window and gazed out at the rain, his back as stiff and straight as his principles. ''Let's just say it was coincidence.''

''I don't believe in coincidence.''

''Call it what you like. We were both at the public library because we're looking for the same thing— information on Max Thorne's murder.''

''Isn't Atlanta quite a ways out of your jurisdiction?''

Dylan nodded, unwilling to tell her the other reason he was after Thorne's killer. ''As a lawman, I have knowledge, thanks to you, that relates to a crime that I think I can solve. Anything I uncover, I'll turn over to the Atlanta homicide division. I don't like killers running loose.''

She wrinkled her attractive face in puzzlement, and he remembered how her lips had tasted the night of the Apple Festival dance. He used all his self-restraint now to keep from kissing her again.

"What about your job in Casey's Cove?" she asked.

He shrugged. "I took vacation time."

"Whew, talk about a busman's holiday." She studied him as if she knew he'd left out a large part of his motive.

He wanted to tell her his whole plan. His heart had sunk to his boots when he'd watched her enter the air terminal on Monday and had realized he might never see her again. He could only hope that Michael Johnson had taken the false lead and headed to San Diego. If not, Jennifer remained in imminent danger. Even if Johnson *had* gone to San Diego, he'd find out soon enough that Jennifer wasn't there, backtrack and stalk her in New York City. No place in the world was big enough to hide from a professional hit man.

Dylan knew her only hope was to neutralize Crutchfield by placing him behind bars. His plan had been to come to Atlanta, find the evidence needed to effect the attorney's arrest, and then write Jennifer in New York, telling her to come home to Casey's Cove.

To come home to *him*.

In spite of her irritating predilection for telling falsehoods, he couldn't erase the woman from his mind. His main reason for coming to Atlanta was to get her back.

But he couldn't admit to her that he cared, because he couldn't trust his own feelings. Not yet. Not until he learned whether the affection he'd sensed from her was genuine or just another of her many deceptions.

He pulled himself from his reflections to find her staring at him curiously.

"What did you turn up on the Thorne case?" he asked.

She pointed to her backpack. "I copied every article I could find, but I haven't had time to read through them yet."

He gestured toward the rain beating against the windowpane. "Today's not good for much else. Want some help?"

"That would be great." She extracted the copies, a legal pad and pencils, and placed them on the table by the window. "With your expertise, you might pick up on something significant I might overlook."

He couldn't help smiling at her enthusiasm. "Let's just say two heads are better than one, especially when it comes to investigations."

He sat opposite her at the dilapidated table, took half the articles, and began to read. Jennifer settled into the chair across from him and perused the other half of the stack. Every now and then, she scribbled notes on the legal pad. With Jennifer only an arm's length away, he enjoyed the intimacy of the tiny room, warm and dry with the rain pounding the roof. He noted her green eyes focused on the pages, her delectable pink tongue sometimes visible at the corner of her tantalizing mouth, and had to force himself to concentrate on the articles about Max Thorne's murder.

About an hour later, she rose and took the teapot into the kitchen for a refill. "Find anything helpful?" she asked when she returned.

He laid down the article he was reading and rubbed his aching eyes. "Nothing that points to the major piece of the puzzle that's missing."

"What's that?"

He stretched his arms above his head to ease the tension in his shoulders, then gratefully accepted a fresh cup of tea. "Motive."

"I *know* Crutchfield killed him."

"Yes, but we don't know *why*. Crutchfield, if your recollections are accurate, had the means—a gun— and the opportunity—the meeting with Thorne in his office. But if we intend to prove our case against your former boss, we have to know what made him decide to blow his biggest client to kingdom come."

She closed her eyes, as if remembering. "Their meetings had always been friendly, until that final one."

"Did you hear any of the specifics of their argument that night?"

She opened her eyes and cast him an apologetic glance. "I was trying *not* to eavesdrop. All I can remember is Thorne screaming, 'you had no right,' and calling the boss some nasty names I won't repeat. Crutchfield just laughed at him, an evil-sounding laugh. A couple of seconds later, I heard gunfire."

"What you think was gunfire," he corrected her.

Her expression drooped. "Don't you believe me?"

"I wouldn't be here if I didn't. But that's the response the homicide detectives will give you, unless we can come up with concrete proof."

She twisted her mouth in a cynical grin. "You'd think two bullets in Max Thorne's heart would be enough to corroborate my theory."

"We cops are a distrustful bunch. We need lots of convincing evidence before we throw a man in jail."

Jennifer raked slender fingers through hair that had dried into a mass of blond ringlets. He remembered the picture Michael Johnson had shown him of her with long red hair and freckles spattered across the bridge of her nose and her cheeks, a glamorous photo that made her look like a model. She was the most attractive woman he'd ever seen. And an expert at disguise. And deceit. Yet here he sat in her living room, taking his hard-earned vacation time to follow her on a wild-goose chase. What had happened to his common sense?

"So, Dick Tracy, what do we do next?"

Her teasing voice jerked him from his reverie. "Let's review what we know about Max Thorne."

She picked up the legal pad and scanned her notes. "He was forty-five when he died. Married with two teenaged children. A millionaire several times over since his worldwide delivery service went public."

"Money problems?"

She shook her head. "None that the office was aware of. He was Crutchfield's biggest account, a real cash cow. The boss always rolled out the red carpet when Thorne appeared.''

Dylan thought for a moment. "Had Crutchfield screwed up somehow? Bungled the account and was trying to hide his mistakes from Thorne?"

"It's possible, but if there was a problem, no one else in the office was aware of it. And I'd have known if Crutchfield was hiding a paper trail. I handled all the documents."

Dylan shoved away from the table and paced the floor of the living room. "We need a two-pronged approach to our investigation. One, to discover Crutchfield's motive. The other, to find physical evidence that connects him to Thorne's murder."

She settled in an overstuffed chair, draped a denim-clad leg across the arm, and swung her bare foot, a pose that threatened to scatter his concentration. "If Crutchfield wasn't covering his own mistakes, what could his motive have been?"

"Revenge, money, ambition—"

"Jealousy?"

"Is Crutchfield married?"

She shook her head. "He doesn't even have a steady girlfriend. But I was thinking of professional jealousy. Crutchfield loved the limelight. When Thorne's company stock skyrocketed, Max became Atlanta society's golden boy."

"Could be the reason," Dylan admitted. "I've heard of stranger motives."

"Such as?"

"I read about a case in Detroit where one man killed another because his feet smelled."

"You're kidding."

"In another, a woman skewered her husband with a barbecue fork because he overcooked her steak."

Jennifer shook her head. "If Crutchfield's motive is that bizarre, we'll never figure it out."

"Those examples were of stupid people, both drunk at the time. Was your boss drinking that night?"

"He sounded sober, and I've never known him to overindulge. He's the kind of man who always likes to be in control."

"And since he's not a stupid man, we'll probably find his motive a logical one, at least to a killer's mind."

She pointed to the newspaper articles. "These have been no help. What do we do next?"

He glanced out the window. The rain had stopped and the reappearing sun hung below the clouds in the western sky. "There's still daylight left. I'd like to get a look at Crutchfield. How far are we from his office?"

"Not far. But you'll never see him there unless you go inside. He takes the elevator directly to the parking garage. You might catch him at his townhouse. It's just a few blocks from his office."

Disinclined to leave her now that he'd found her again, he asked, "Ever been on a stakeout?"

"I've seen them on TV and in the movies. Does that count?"

"Close enough. I have a thermos in the car. Can you make coffee, extra strong?"

"Sure, and while it's brewing, I'll find some dry shoes."

He sprinted down the stairs to his truck, grabbed the thermos and returned. Jennifer was lacing sneakers over thick white socks. She had changed her sweatshirt for a white blouse whose crisp collar peeked above the neckline of a pale yellow sweater, a perfect foil for her golden hair.

"Better bring a jacket, too," he warned. "The temperature's diving."

A few minutes later, they were in the truck with a filled thermos and a blanket borrowed from Jennifer's bedroom in case their stakeout lasted into the night.

"Where's the nearest pizza place?" he asked.

She directed him to one nearby where he ordered two large pizzas to go while she waited in the truck.

"We've got coffee, pizza and a blanket," she said when he returned, "but no binoculars or high-tech listening devices like I've seen in the movies."

"No doughnuts, either," he answered with a pseudo-serious expression, "but somehow we'll manage."

"Turn left," she directed as he drove from the parking lot. "Crutchfield's apartment is about a mile south of here."

Traffic was thickening as the rush hour approached, but as they reached the posh suburb of Crutchfield's townhouse, hardly a car passed them.

"This isn't good," Dylan said. "In this neighborhood, my truck will stick out like a sore thumb."

"Maybe the neighbors will think you're a trades-man working late."

"As long as the Neighborhood Watch doesn't call the cops on us, we should be okay."

"That's it." Jennifer pointed to a row of contem-porary townhouses. "His place is at the far end."

Dylan parked the truck across the street in the shade of a large oak, a spot that would be in almost total darkness once night fell. From the cab, they had a clear view of Crutchfield's parking space and front door.

"Now what?" Jennifer asked.

"We wait for Crutchfield to come home from work so I can get a good look at him."

"Will looking at him tell you anything?"

Dylan nodded. "You can judge a great deal of a man's character by the way he moves and carries himself."

"But not enough to brand him as a killer?"

"No, but if we follow him around for a while, determine his favorite routes and the places he fre-quents, we might have a clue to where he may have stashed hard evidence."

"Like what?"

"Like the gun he used to kill Thorne, or the blood-stained carpet from his office."

He was having a hard time concentrating. The compact atmosphere of the truck's interior put him too close to Jennifer. The faint scent of honeysuckle tickled his nose, and he was all too aware he had only to reach out to touch her. And he *wanted* to touch her. He wanted to kiss her until she responded with the fervor she'd shown she was capable of. He wanted to hold her, protect her....

He wrenched his thoughts from that dangerous direction. He was too fond of the pretty woman beside him. Not a good idea when he knew so little about her. His instincts warned him that she still held secrets, that he'd only peeled back the first thin layer of the complex puzzle that was Jennifer Reid. That surface layer was attractive, seductive even, but as a student of human nature, he'd learned long ago that appealing appearances could hide a rotten center. He didn't believe he'd discover that with Jennifer, but until he had uncovered her secrets, he'd be smart to keep his distance.

He decided to push her, nudge her memories while they waited. "You don't seem to remember much about Casey's Cove when we were kids."

"Sure I do." She gazed out the window as if avoiding his eyes. "I wouldn't have come back if I hadn't."

"What's your favorite memory?"

She shrugged. "There's so many. Swimming in the lake, hiking in the mountains—"

"What do you remember about me, Tommy Bennett and the other kids?"

She turned toward him, and in the dusky light, he could read the panic in her eyes. "I...uh..."

"You don't have any memories of us, do you?" The cop in him wondered why, and at the same time he hated himself for the agony he was causing her.

"No, I don't remember anything," she admitted.

"Call me cynical, but I find that very odd."

"I don't blame you." Even in the dim light, he could see the vivid flush that spread from her collar to the roots of her thick hair.

"I've never shared the reason with anyone."

"What reason?"

She took a deep breath, almost hyperventilating. "Aunt Emily."

"What about her?"

Jennifer turned away again, as if ashamed to face him. "She was emotionally abusive. I spent years in therapy after she died. My psychiatrist claims the memories I've repressed will return when I'm ready to face them. That's another reason I came back to Casey's Cove, to jog them loose. So far it hasn't worked."

He was torn between pity and disbelief. She'd lied to him so often, would he ever trust anything she said? But why tell lies about her childhood, especially about a topic so obviously painful to her?

"I'm sorry I put you on the spot." Only time would reveal whether she told the truth, *if* she was able to reclaim her lost experiences of their shared youth and relate them to him. In the meantime, he was back where he'd started, unsure of her veracity and keeping his own emotional distance.

Over an hour dragged by. The sun set, the street lights came on and darkness settled over the suburban street. And still no sign of Larry Crutchfield.

"Hungry?" he asked Jennifer.

"Hungry enough to eat cold pizza," she replied.

He had to admire her fortitude. Other women would have complained long ago about the boredom, the cold, the discomfort of sitting so long doing nothing. She hadn't grumbled once.

He passed her a handful of paper napkins and the pizza box. "You think Crutchfield's working late?"

"More likely he has a social engagement." She selected a large slice and returned the box to him. "Sometimes he changed into his tux at the office if he was going out."

Dylan helped himself to pizza. "So we may be in for a long wait."

A Lincoln Town Car drove slowly past. "They're either looking for an address or wondering what we're doing here," Jennifer said.

The car passed without slowing further and turned at the next street.

"I've thought about contacting the homicide detectives who handled Max's case." Dylan wiped tomato sauce from the corner of his mouth. "Maybe they'll share what they know with us."

"Go to the police?" Her voice slid up an octave. "Why? We haven't any proof. Wouldn't you rather see what we can turn up on our own first? Obviously the Atlanta cops have reached a dead end or they'd have made an arrest."

"Maybe they have something they could link to Crutchfield if they know he's a suspect." Curious at her reluctance to bring in the authorities, he studied her face.

Her expression was barely visible in the deep shadows, but he could see the alarm that flickered over her features. "You can go if you wish," she said, "but leave me out of it."

"But you're the one with the information."

Her expression closed up tighter than a miser's fist, as if she were afraid the slightest nuance might give away details she wanted to remain hidden.

"Let's see what we find on our own first," she said, too casually.

He suppressed the urge to grab her and shake her secrets from her. Knowing Jennifer, she'd only clam up tighter under pressure. But his imagination was running wild. What could she be hiding that she was so afraid of disclosing? Was *she* somehow involved in Max Thorne's murder? His intuition told him she wasn't a criminal. And Miss Bessie's intuition, the best in the cove, had sensed only goodness in Jennifer Reid. If he could put Crutchfield behind bars, maybe then she might confide in him.

And what happens if you don't like what she tells you? an inner voice demanded.

He'd cross that bridge when he came to it.

Between them, they emptied the thermos of coffee and finished off the pizza as the hours dragged by. Dylan draped the blanket over their knees and drew Jennifer closer in an effort to keep warm. Ice formed on the windshield, and twice Dylan turned on the engine and the defroster to clear it away.

He was enjoying the warmth of her curled against his side. This was a pleasure he could definitely get used to.

Suddenly she sat upright and pulled away. "That's Crutchfield's midnight-blue Mercedes."

The luxury car pulled into the parking space in front of the townhouse. A man in a tuxedo climbed out of the driver's seat and circled the car to the passenger side. Although the parking area was poorly lit, Jennifer immediately recognized the tall, well-built man in his mid-thirties as her former boss. He moved with elegance in his custom-tailored evening clothes, and the reflected moonlight made his blond hair appear silver. She didn't have to see his eyes to remember their coldness and the hatred they'd projected when he'd caught sight of her in the Chicago train station.

Crutchfield opened the passenger door.

A pair of long, slender legs appeared as a woman exited the car. A long full-length velvet cloak with a hood concealed her from view, except when the garment parted to reveal a silver lamé cocktail dress that barely covered the woman's thighs. Crutchfield took her in his arms and kissed her, a deep, probing kiss that continued for several minutes. The woman's hood fell back, but all Jennifer could see was a crown of dark hair.

"That's pretty intense for a man who has no steady girl," Dylan observed. "Do you recognize the woman?"

The couple broke apart and headed for the front door. In the glow of the porch light, the woman turned and faced the street while Crutchfield unlocked the door.

Jennifer gasped in surprise. "That's Elissa Thorne. Max Thorne's wife."

Chapter Eight

"Not exactly the grieving widow, is she?" Sarcasm lent a harsh edge to Dylan's rich voice. "What's it been, five whole months since her husband's murder?"

Although Jennifer knew Crutchfield couldn't see her in the dark, remembering their confrontation in Chicago, she slid lower in her seat. "Looks like Crutchfield's good at consolation. Elissa seems—uh, enthusiastic."

"Maybe it's not consolation."

Shaken by the bitterness in his voice, she turned from the preoccupied couple to Dylan. "What are you saying?"

His brown eyes burned like dark coals in the dim light. "Could be Crutchfield and Mrs. Thorne were an item *before* Max's death."

"You think Crutchfield killed Thorne to steal his wife?" As much as she disliked her former boss, she found the idea of that deception hard to swallow. "Wouldn't a divorce have been a lot less messy?"

"Probably." The sharpness hadn't left his voice. "But if Mrs. Thorne stood to inherit *all* of her late husband's estate, a divorce with a maximum fifty-fifty split of assets wouldn't be nearly as profitable.''

Censure and disgust seemed to ooze from Dylan's pores. Jennifer never wanted him to disapprove of her as thoroughly as he did Crutchfield, but she knew that time would come, especially when she revealed all she'd been hiding from him since the day they met. And that day was coming, sooner than she liked to think.

"You know Crutchfield," Dylan said. "Is he capable of killing for love?"

Jennifer thought back to the man who had been her boss all those months. He'd been ambitious, self-centered, cold—and money-hungry. "I can't see him putting himself in jeopardy for love. But if the stakes were high enough, he might risk murder for profit."

Turned toward Dylan, she could view the street behind them through the rear window. Suddenly, headlights appeared a block away, and the blue flash of a light bar lit the top of an approaching police car. It slowed as it neared and pulled to the curb behind them.

Dylan glanced in the rearview mirror. "Looks like we'll be bringing the police into our investigation whether you're ready or not."

"Not necessarily." Thinking quickly, she flung her arms around his neck. "Just follow my lead."

With a boldness she hadn't known she possessed, she pressed her lips to his and wound her fingers through his hair. He stiffened as if in surprise, even as his arms reflexively closed around her. Shifting nearer, she pressed against him.

She felt his muscles relax, and he drew her closer and returned her kiss. He tasted of coffee, sunshine and a distinctive masculine flavor, and his lips were warm, even in the frigid night air. A vein in his neck pulsed beneath her fingers, and his heart beat against her breasts. She breathed the air that he exhaled and sensed her pulse synchronize with his, as if they had become one.

With her senses operating at maximum input, she forgot the approaching officer, forgot her many deceptions, forgot Larry Crutchfield's threats as happiness swelled inside her. This was where she belonged, in the strong arms of Dylan Blackburn, a rugged, uncomplicated man of the mountains, steeped in solid principles and dedicated to protecting and serving the people he loved.

"Jennifer," he murmured when he came up for air, and the name on his lips sounded like a blessing.

A sudden tapping on the driver's window broke the spell. She pulled away, sorry that the moment had ended, shaken by the intensity of her feelings. She looked at Dylan to see if he had been affected as much as she, but he had turned away to roll down his window.

The powerful beam of a flashlight temporarily blinded her before the police officer lowered the torch to his side. As her eyes adjusted again to the darkness, she could see the tall, black cop who leaned down until his face was framed by the window.

"Don't you folks have a home to go to?" Raised

eyebrows and the irony in his voice left no doubt that he'd witnessed their kiss.

Dylan opened his mouth to speak, but Jennifer beat him to the punch. She couldn't allow him to give away the real reason they were parked along Crutchfield's street. That information would give rise to other questions—questions she didn't want to answer until the moment was right.

"Of course we have a home, officer." She gave him her Atlanta address. "But we like to come here and dream about which of these places we'll live in when we win the lottery."

The cop looked at her as if she was a few bricks short of a load and turned to Dylan. "You got ID?"

"Sure."

Dylan removed his driver's license from his wallet, and Jennifer glanced across the street. Crutchfield and Mrs. Thorne had interrupted their passionate embrace long enough to stare at the truck and the police car, lights flashing, behind it. Jennifer prayed the darkness of the cab kept her unrecognizable. She was relying on Crutchfield's reluctance to inconvenience himself to help others to keep him on his side of the street.

"There isn't a law against daydreaming, is there?" she asked.

"Sorry, but we can't be too careful. We've had several break-ins in this neighborhood recently, so we're keeping close check of any suspicious persons."

"Do we *look* like burglars?" she asked.

Dylan shot her a warning glance that under different circumstances might have caused her to cease all comments, and the officer ignored her. "Step out of the car, please, Mr. Blackburn."

Jennifer groaned and slid lower in her seat. If they ended up at the station, she'd have to answer those tough questions, whether she wanted to or not.

"We're not thieves," she insisted.

"Jennifer, please, let me handle this." Dylan kept his hands on the steering wheel where the cop could see them. "Before I get out, officer, I want you to know I'm a policeman from Casey's Cove, North Carolina, and I'm carrying a weapon in a holster at my back."

"Step out slowly and raise your hands," the cop said.

Dylan climbed out of the truck. Another police car approached from the opposite direction, made a U-turn and parked behind the first cruiser. The driver, a second officer, advanced toward the truck. "What have you got, Hayden?"

"Don't know yet. I'm going to run the ID and tags through the computer." The black cop patted Dylan down, removed his gun and took it and his driver's license back to his cruiser.

"We haven't done anything wrong," Jennifer said heatedly, "unless necking has been declared a crime."

The other cop, a stocky, middle-aged white man, gazed in the window. "Stay in the truck, ma'am. Just keep your hands where I can see them."

Jennifer glanced across the street. Larry Crutchfield had left Elissa Thorne by the front door of his townhouse and was heading up the sidewalk toward the curb. Jennifer jerked around to hide her face.

"What's going on, officers?" he called across the street.

Jennifer squirmed at his proximity. His smug, patronizing tone hadn't mellowed in the five months since she'd last seen him.

Don't let him cross the street, she prayed.

"Nothing we can't handle," the stocky officer shouted back. "You live here?"

"In the first townhouse."

"Then I suggest you go on inside. We're almost finished, and we don't need an audience."

Jennifer smiled. The officer had put Crutchfield in his place, a situation that was certain to make her old boss seethe. She heard his retreating footsteps ringing in the crisp, cold air. When she glanced across the street again, Crutchfield and Mrs. Thorne were entering the building.

Dylan stood silently with the second officer while the first sat in his cruiser, talking on the radio. After at least ten long minutes, the black officer approached and returned Dylan's gun and license.

"Your story and ID check out," he said. "Since you were on duty the nights of our other break-ins, you can't be our burglar."

"Of course not," Jennifer said, her voice hitting a high note of indignation. "Dylan's the best cop I know."

The black cop regarded her through narrowed eyes, then turned to Dylan. "Your girlfriend's a looker all right. But I can't understand why you were making out here in the cold, when she has a place of her own.''

Jennifer pretended offense. "You *obviously* have no sense of romance or adventure.''

The stocky officer laughed. "Yeah, Hayden, didn't you ever hear of an arm-strong heater? A bit of nooky can warm up a truck cab in no time flat.''

Jennifer avoided Dylan's gaze. He was glaring at her as if he'd like to leave her out in the cold. Alone.

Hayden scratched his chin. "Guess those arm-strong heaters were before my time.''

"Green as you are,'' the older officer said with a laugh, "*everything* was before your time.''

"Do you mind,'' Jennifer said, "if we get going? It's freezing out here.''

The stocky cop nodded at Dylan, and he climbed into the truck. The cop approached and spoke through the window. "Just some friendly advice, Blackburn. If you intend to marry this woman, don't count on getting a word in edgewise. She's got quite a mouth on her.''

Jennifer sputtered in outrage, but Dylan rolled up the window before she could fire a return volley. Her outrage increased when she noted his wide grin, but she was smart enough to keep quiet.

The cops returned to their respective cars and waited for Dylan to leave. Dylan turned to her, smile gone, eyes blazing. "Why did you do that?''

"Do what?''

"Make up that cock-and-bull story of dreaming about houses and winning the lottery?''

The memory of his kiss wilted beneath his displeasure. "We had to tell them something."

"What about the truth?" A muscle in his jaw twitched in anger. He twisted the key in the ignition with such force she feared he'd break it. "That's always worked for me."

She decided a strong offense was her best defense. "What harm did I do? Did I commit a crime? No. Did I save us from hours of explanation and a trip to the station? Yes. So what's the problem?"

He shook his head and put the truck in gear. "You lied. And I went along with you. That's the problem."

"Look," she said calmly, "You showed them your ID. You didn't lie about your identity. And we haven't broken the law."

He pulled away from the curb and headed down the dark street, then flicked her a look she couldn't read. "There must have been something illegal about that kiss."

She felt her face flush with the memory. "It was just a diversion."

"It was diverting, all right. You're good at that, aren't you?"

She purposely misunderstood. "Kissing?"

With a heavy sigh of frustration, he shook his head. "Diversions, deceptions. Is anything you've ever told me the truth?"

"Yes." She crossed her heart and held up her right hand. "I swear that I truly detest Miss Bessie's cinnamon rolls."

When he laughed, she exhaled with relief.

"Now *that* I believe," he said.

"So, Dick Tracy, what do we do now?"

"What any good detective on stakeout would do. We find Elissa Thorne's address and wait there to see if she spends the night with Crutchfield."

"What if the cops stop us again?"

"Do me a favor," he said. "If they do, let *me* do the talking this time."

She settled back into the seat and tucked the blanket around her knees. All she could think of was kissing him again.

And all the reasons why she shouldn't.

DYLAN KNEADED the lumpy pillow with his fists, folded it in half and crammed it beneath his head. Staring at the ceiling with sleepless eyes, he thought he might as well get up, but he didn't want to waken Jennifer, asleep in the next room.

They had returned to her lodgings at five-thirty that morning after watching Larry Crutchfield deliver Elissa Thorne to her door. No passionate embraces that trip, however. Mrs. Thorne must have been afraid her children or the neighbors would be watching. Crutchfield didn't even get out of his car.

Upon returning to her apartment, Jennifer had offered Dylan a bed on the sofa in her living room and retired to the bedroom to catch up on the missed night's sleep. But he hadn't been able to close his eyes. His thoughts bounced back and forth like a ball in a tennis match. Remembering Jennifer's unexpected kiss sent his adrenaline pumping. Then he'd recall her motives for kissing him, and his spirits would plummet. She hadn't kissed him out of love, or even lust, but solely to mislead the Atlanta cops who'd stopped to question them. This woman could give lessons in deception to Mata Hari.

Although her motives had been ulterior, he couldn't deny the power of that kiss. In spite of his reluctance to deceive his fellow officers, he had wanted their embrace to last forever—and then segue into something more. He'd never responded to a woman so totally. Jennifer had felt as if she'd been made for his lips, for his arms only.

Then his thoughts bounced back to her facile lies, her effortless delusions, and he wanted to hold his head and groan with frustration. How could he possibly be falling in love with a woman of whom he so thoroughly disapproved?

Because she has so many qualities you admire, his heart told him. *Courage, intelligence, a sense of humor.*

She's a natural-born con artist, his intellect retorted.

"You awake?" Jennifer peered over the back of the sofa at him.

"Speak of the devil," he murmured.

"What?" Her cheeks glowed pink, as if she'd just scrubbed them, and her tousled curls were held back by a green ribbon that matched her eyes. She smelled of soap and her distinctive honeysuckle fragrance and looked more delicious than ever, which didn't help his morning disposition.

"Yeah, I'm awake," he said. "What are you doing up so soon? You can't have been asleep more than an hour.''

''I couldn't rest,'' she admitted with a smile that quirked the corners of her mouth. ''I know what we need to do next.''

He knew what he *wanted* to do next. He wanted to kiss those luscious lips again.

''I thought I was supposed to be Dick Tracy,'' he said with a fake grumble.

''You are,'' she agreed sweetly, ''and I'm your trusty assistant.''

He lifted himself on his elbows to push his face closer to hers. ''Trusty? I'm always wondering what trouble you'll cause next.''

Just as he was tempted to grab her, she spun away and went into the kitchen. She was wearing an over-sized T-shirt that hung to her thighs and left her slender legs enticingly bare.

''We'll have to go back to the library and get copies of news photos of Elissa Thorne,'' she shouted over running water as she filled the coffeepot.

Sitting up, he dragged his fingers through his hair and tugged on his shoes, wondering how anyone could be so damned perky after only one hour's sleep. He stood, crossed the room and watched while she made coffee. If he couldn't sleep, he might as well humor her.

''Okay, trusty assistant, once we have the pictures, then what?''

''I remember all the little out-of-the-way restaurants where Crutchfield eats. He had me make reservations for him. Usually he told me who he was taking, but sometimes he'd just say make the reservations for two, that he was meeting a client.'' She flipped the switch on the coffeemaker and took mugs from the cabinet. "I figure we can divide up the list, go to the restaurants and ask the waiters if they've ever seen Elissa there with him."

"But we already know he's involved with Mrs. Thorne." Dylan, his brain badly in need of sleep, was having trouble following her.

"But we don't know for how long. Maybe they were frequenting one or more of those restaurants for months before Max died."

The pieces of her explanation finally clicked into place, and he gazed at her admiringly. "You *are* a wonder."

"Thanks." She flushed with pleasure at his compliment, blushing so prettily he was seized once more with the overwhelming urge to kiss her again.

"Mind if I take a shower?" he asked.

Her expression fell. "I'm afraid I used all the hot water."

"No problem."

He headed for the bathroom. This morning, a long, cold shower was exactly what he needed.

SIX HOURS and eighteen restaurants later, they met back at Jennifer's apartment.

"Any luck?" Dylan asked.

The picture of dejection, she collapsed onto the sofa, pulled off her sneakers and massaged her feet. "Zip."

"Me neither," he admitted in frustration. "Some

remembered seeing Crutchfield and Mrs. Thorne in their restaurants, but never together.''

Jennifer stretched her bare feet in front of her and wiggled her toes. "Crutchfield must have been too smart to meet his lover in the Atlanta area. Guess he figured somebody would see them and spill the beans to Max.''

"Maybe somebody did," Dylan suggested. "A tip-off could have been the reason for that after-hours meeting in Crutchfield's office that got Max killed.''

"But we have no proof. And we can't put Crutchfield behind bars without proof.''

Dylan sat in the overstuffed chair across from her and rubbed his stomach. The fast-food burrito he'd swallowed too quickly at lunchtime was attacking his insides with a jackhammer. "They had to meet somewhere. Did Crutchfield make any regular trips out of town?''

Eyes sparkling, she sat up and slammed her feet to the floor. "You are brilliant!''

"Clue me in.''

"There's this quaint bed and breakfast in Madison. Crutchfield had me make reservations for him there at least once a month. He said he had to get out of Atlanta overnight every few weeks to 'decompress' from the stress of work. Maybe that's where he and Elissa had their rendezvous.''

"How far is Madison from here?''

She wrinkled her nose, apparently a habit when she was trying to remember. "It's a straight shot east on I-20 about sixty-five miles. Takes about an hour.''

Dylan thought of his aching stomach. "Maybe a phone call would be easier."

Shaking her head, she grinned. "You're losing it, Dick Tracy. Can't show the innkeepers photos over the phone."

"You're right. And I doubt they registered under their real names. But I have one request before we leave."

She assumed the guarded expression he'd noted so often. "What request?"

"Do you have any antacid? My stomach's killing me."

Concern replaced her wariness, and she hurried into the kitchen and pulled a bottle of fast-dissolve tablets from a cabinet. He accepted them with thanks, chewed and swallowed.

Jennifer hastily pulled on her socks and sneakers. "You want me to drive until you're feeling better?"

"I came all the way to Atlanta to track a murderer for you. I even sat all night in the cold on your behalf. But a man's got to draw the line somewhere. I won't let you drive my truck."

She pretended to be hurt. "You Southern boys are all alike. Guess I'm just lucky you didn't bring your huntin' dog to sleep on my sofa with you."

He thought of all the country songs he'd heard with lyrics about a man's truck and his dogs. Most songs contained another key ingredient—a broken heart. And Jennifer Reid had all the qualifications of a heartbreaker. Good looks, sex appeal and a propensity for avoiding the truth. He had to keep on his guard if he wanted to return to Casey's Cove with his heart intact.

AFTER A DRIVE of just over an hour, they reached the small town of Madison with its charming streets of antebellum and Victorian houses. The bed and breakfast sat on a hill outside town, looking like a movie set for *Gone with the Wind*. A winding road between towering pecan trees led to the three-story house. Its white columns and clapboards were covered with a creeping vine singed scarlet by frost, and drifts of golden leaves from the ancient maples and hickories dappled the lawn. Rows of rocking chairs graced the wide front porch, and lamps glowed from every window to welcome guests in the late-afternoon gloom.

Dylan parked the truck in a lot shielded from the house by a hedge of evergreens. Several cars and sport utility vehicles filled the spaces. He hopped from the truck and opened Jennifer's door.

"Looks like this place does a booming business," he said with a nod toward the crowded lot.

"Let's hope they haven't had so many guests they can't identify Crutchfield and Mrs. Thorne."

Their feet crunched on the gravel surface until they reached the brick path that led to wide double doors at the entrance. Garlands of fall leaves, dried corn husks and Indian corn tied with gold velvet bows decorated the doors and windows of the first floor. The faint strains of a string quartet emanated from the building.

As they reached the entrance, the doors opened and a balding, middle-aged man dressed in a plaid shirt, beige slacks, a cardigan sweater and tasseled loafers stood waiting. "Welcome, folks. You're just in time for afternoon tea."

"Are you the manager?" Dylan asked.

"Tom Putnam, innkeeper, at your service. Do you have reservations?"

"No—" Dylan began.

"Then you're in luck," Putnam said. "We have one room left for the weekend."

Dylan hesitated. He'd wanted to ask his questions and leave, but now that he'd seen the place, he realized the host would treat his inquiries with more respect if Dylan were a paying guest.

"That's great." Dylan turned to Jennifer and signaled her with a look to play along with him. "Isn't it, dear?"

She twisted her lips in an ironic smile. "Whatever you say, sweetheart."

They followed Putnam into the entrance hall. The innkeeper moved behind a counter of carved mahogany and slid a register across its smooth surface toward Dylan. "Your room overlooks the rear gardens and the lake. The view is impressive this time of year with the fall foliage at its peak."

"I'm sure we'll love it," Jennifer said.

Dylan was grateful she'd said it with a straight face. Once they reached the room, he'd have some heavy explaining to do. The last thing he wanted was for her to misunderstand his motives.

"Will you be paying in cash or by credit card?" the host asked.

"We can only stay one night," Dylan said. "How much will that be?"

Putnam quoted the price, and Dylan fought to keep his shock from showing. He rarely carried that much cash. It was almost a week's pay.

"Put it on my card." He handed his card to the host.

While Putnam was checking his credit status, Dylan noticed Jennifer nonchalantly flipping backwards in the guest register, so deeply engrossed, she'd missed his conversation with the innkeeper. When Putnam turned back toward them, she returned quickly to the appropriate page and Dylan signed.

Putnam returned Dylan's card and handed him a room key. "Thank you, Mr. and Mrs. Blackburn. I hope you'll enjoy your stay. Would you like to see your room now or join us for tea in the front parlor?"

"Tea, please," Jennifer said before Dylan could comment. "I'm starving."

"Follow me."

Putnam led the way through double doors into an enormous formal room with floor-to-ceiling windows draped in heavy brocade, French antique furniture and a roaring fire in a marble fireplace. A buffet table set with a silver tea service, silver platters of sandwiches and tiered crystal cake stands stood along one wall. Several guests helped themselves to the refreshments while others lounged in the many sofas and chairs scattered throughout the room.

"Enjoy yourselves," Putnam said, "and if you want a recommendation for dining out tonight, I'll be happy to assist."

He nodded to a few of the guests and returned to the entry hall.

"How much is this setting us back?" Jennifer whispered to Dylan.

"Enough that I might have to mortgage my truck," he murmured.

Her gasp was audible above the muted classical music flowing from a hidden sound system.

"I'm kidding," Dylan assured her.

"I'm not." She tugged on his elbow. "We have to get out of here, fast."

He allowed her to pull him toward the door. "What's gotten into you?"

"Don't look now," she warned, "but Crutchfield and Mrs. Thorne are sitting at a table by the rear window."

Chapter Nine

Heart pounding, Jennifer grabbed Dylan's hand and pulled him across the foyer toward the staircase. "Don't let them see us," she whispered fiercely.

At the front desk, Putnam lifted his head from the book he was reading. "Anything wrong?"

"Jennifer's decided she wants to see our room," Dylan said. "Any chance of having tea sent up?"

"I'll have a tray delivered immediately," Putnam said.

Jennifer yanked Dylan's hand impatiently, and he followed her up the elegantly carved, curving staircase to the second floor.

"For what Putnam's charging us, he can afford to have tea delivered, accompanied by a brass band," Dylan grumbled.

While Jennifer shifted anxiously from foot to foot and kept watch down the hall, Dylan turned the ancient key in the old-fashioned lock. As soon as he had the door open, she scooted past him.

He entered behind her and closed the door.

Collapsing into a slipper chair by the fireplace, she

fanned her face and waited for her pulse to cease its gallop. "That was close."

"You're sure it was them?"

She grimaced. "I'd know that cold-hearted creep anywhere."

"He didn't see you?"

"He was too busy making goo-goo eyes at Elissa Thorne. Neither one of them spotted me."

Dylan settled into a chair on the other end of the hearth. "At least you were right about their coming here."

She cocked her head and regarded him with a slow smile. "What's the idea of booking this room? You're not trying to seduce me, are you?"

"Why should I try?" His brown eyes twinkled with mischief. "I'll just wait until we meet another cop and let you throw yourself at me again."

Heat inched from her neck to her forehead. She'd never blushed as much in her life as she had since meeting Dylan. "And you registered us as Mr. and Mrs.?"

"I registered under my name only. Let Putnam draw his own conclusions."

"Why *did* you decide to stay?"

Dylan leaned forward, all signs of teasing gone from the rugged lines of his face. "This isn't some flophouse where I can bribe the night clerk with five bucks and learn all about the clientele. I figure Tom Putnam will be more forthcoming with information if we're paying guests."

"Makes sense." She couldn't help feeling disappointed. Although she'd joked about it, she found the prospect of being seduced by Dylan in the intimate elegance of the bed-and-breakfast suite enchanting.

She took her first good look at their accommodation. It was a spacious room with its own bathroom. A huge bay window, filled with a window seat with plump cushions, overlooked the garden. English-rose chintz covered the chairs and the massive canopied bed. Arrangements of fresh roses and peppery carnations scented the room. Cozy, intimate and romantic, the room was everything two people could want, if—

A knock sounded.

"Must be our tea." Dylan rose and opened the door.

A pretty young woman in her early twenties stood in the doorway. Like Tom Putnam, she wore casual slacks and a sweater. She carried an enormous silver tray laden with a porcelain teapot and cups, and plates of sandwiches and cakes.

She placed the tray on a table between their chairs. "If you need anything else, my name's Kyra, and I'm happy to serve you.

"Thanks." Dylan slipped her a tip.

"Have you worked here long?" Jennifer asked before Kyra reached the door.

"Over a year, ma'am."

"Good, then maybe you can help us."

The girl nodded. "That's why I'm here."

Jennifer smiled. "I meant you can help us to remember. We saw a couple downstairs a few minutes ago that I *know* we're supposed to know, but I can't remember their names."

Dylan jumped in. "The man is tall and blond, and the woman with him is slender with dark hair."

Kyra thought for a moment. "That would be Mr. and Mrs. O'Riley."

"O'Riley?" Jennifer jerked in surprise and spilled the tea she was attempting to pour. "Are you sure?"

"Oh, yes, ma'am. They're regulars. They've been coming here since before Thanksgiving last year, about the same time I started working here. They're friends of yours?"

"No," Dylan broke in. "If they're the O'Rileys, they're not who we thought they were."

"Funny how people often aren't who you think they are. Enjoy your tea." Kyra went out and closed the door.

Dylan selected a dainty chicken salad sandwich from the plate. "The O'Rileys? You sure you recognized Crutchfield and Mrs. Thorne?"

She clutched the teapot to stop her hands from shaking and poured him a cup of tea. "I'm absolutely positive. If Crutchfield was seeing Mrs. Thorne on the sly, he wouldn't register under his real name. Besides, O'Riley was the name of one of his secretaries, so it's a logical alias."

Lost in thought, Dylan chewed his sandwich. Jennifer's own hunger had disappeared. Events were moving too fast for her. She would have to tell Dylan the truth—and soon—or he would find out on his own. If the latter happened, he might never speak to her again.

She picked up her cup and saucer. "When I was flipping through the register downstairs, I didn't see

Crutchfield's name, but O'Riley popped up several times."

Sinking into a chair, Dylan nodded. "Then we've got our motive. All we need now is physical evidence to link Crutchfield to the crime."

"All *you* need now is some sleep." Her heart ached at the sight of his exhaustion. "The circles under your eyes have circles of their own."

"You're as sleep-deprived as I am." He glanced around the cozy room as if taking it in for the first time. "Looks like we have a problem. One bed, no sofa."

"No problem. Since I doubt any cops will be breaking into our room, you can sleep next to me without fear of attack." She forced an easy smile to hide emotions running rampant at the thought of spending the night beside him.

He hesitated, and she wondered if he was having the same thoughts. "I could sleep on the window seat," he offered.

"And end up knotted like a pretzel? The bed's big enough for both of us."

Swallowing the last bite of a piece of cake, he stood and stretched. "For once, I'm not going to argue with you. I'm dead on my feet."

He went into the adjoining bathroom and closed the door. Knowing they wouldn't be going out for dinner, Jennifer picked up a sandwich. The delicious chicken salad restored her appetite, and she was munching happily on spice cake when Dylan came out of the bath.

"At least they include all the amenities," he ob-

served. "Toothbrushes, toothpaste, shampoo, dispos-
able razors."

"Wonder how many guests arrive as we did, without baggage?" She dusted crumbs from her hands
and tried to keep from staring. He'd stripped to his
jeans with bare feet and a provocatively bare chest.
Well-muscled and tanned, except for the circles under his eyes he looked even better than he had the
first day she'd met him.

"At least Putnam was polite enough not to comment on our lack of luggage." Dylan walked to the
right side of the bed, removed his gun and holster,
and laid them on the bedside table. He sat on the bed
and bounced gingerly a few times.

"Comfy?" Jennifer asked.

He tossed aside the bedspread, lay back on the pile
of pillows edged with Battenburg lace, and clasped
his hands behind his head. "As tired as I am, it could
be a bed of nails, and I wouldn't even notice."

"Would you like something else to eat?"

He didn't answer. Jennifer saw that his eyes were
closed. Mesmerized by the rhythmic rise and fall of
his magnificent chest muscles, she tiptoed to his side
of the bed. He was sound asleep.

She returned to her chair before the fire and poured
herself another cup of tea. When he awoke, she
would tell him the truth. The whole truth. She'd lied
to him in the beginning to protect herself, but ever
since confessing to Dylan about Crutchfield, she'd
been lying to protect Dylan's opinion of her. If she
continued her deception much longer, he'd learn the
truth from someone else. She didn't hold out much

hope of his forgiving her lies, but she stood a better chance at forgiveness if she told him the facts herself.

Sipping the strong, sweet tea, she thought back over the past five months of flight and fear. Now that they had a motive, if she and Dylan could find evidence to convict Crutchfield, her running and her terror would end.

But where could they find the proof they needed?

She walked to the window. The sun had set almost an hour earlier, and colonial lampposts scattered through the grounds cast a soft glow over the garden. Brighter lights illuminated the parking lot, and she caught sight of Crutchfield's midnight-blue Mercedes in a far corner of the lot, barely visible beneath the overhanging branches of a gigantic walnut tree. Except for Dylan's truck and one other car, the rest of the lot was empty. She assumed the other guests had gone into town for dinner. Maybe Crutchfield and Mrs. Thorne had done as she and Dylan had and made a meal of afternoon tea. After all, if the guilty couple had come all this way to be together, why embark back into public again just for a meal?

She glanced over her shoulder at Dylan, so fast asleep a jumbo jet could fly through the room without waking him. As quietly as possible, she dug into her purse for a dark scarf and tied it over her blond curls. Her light-colored sweater would stand out in the darkness, so she slipped into Dylan's dark jacket. After a final check to make certain he was still sleeping, she opened the door slowly, assured herself that the upstairs hall was empty and stepped out.

Wanting to remain unseen on her clandestine

foray, she avoided the main stairs. At the opposite end of the hall, she discovered a stairway that led to the rear door of the house. Within minutes, she was out the door and in the garden.

Glancing up, she could see faint light from the dim lamp she'd left burning gleaming through the uncovered windows of the room where Dylan slept. At the far end of the house, lights glowed behind drawn curtains, and she wondered if that was Crutchfield's room.

She hurried along the garden path to the edge of the parking lot and sprinted across to the Mercedes. First she tried the driver's door. It was locked. The same with the passenger door on the driver's side. Although she knew Crutchfield had probably secured all the doors at once with the car's electric locking system, she refused to give up. She circled the car and was tugging at the passenger door when the sound of footsteps made her pause. Peering around the car, she spotted a man crossing the parking lot toward her.

It was Crutchfield.

She had nowhere to run without being seen. Praying he hadn't already sighted her, she scurried through a thorny hedge that scratched her face and hands, then hid behind the massive trunk of a walnut tree. Her breath came in ragged gasps, and she feared Crutchfield would hear it, even if he couldn't see her.

Pressing her face against the tree's rough bark, she prayed for him to go away. Over the thunder of her own heart, she heard the *thunk* of the electronic locks disengaging on his car, heard a door open, the rustle of a package and then the door slam. The locks engaged again. With any luck, he'd return to his room without discovering her.

"Hey," he suddenly shouted, "you, behind the tree. What are you doing?"

Panic overwhelmed her. Without thinking where she was going, she bolted from behind the tree and headed into the adjoining woods.

Pounding footsteps followed her.

She ran as if her life depended on it. If Crutchfield caught her, he'd kill her—or hold her until Michael Johnson could do his dirty work for him. Running blindly in the darkness, she stumbled over a tree root and fell to her hands and knees. Crutchfield was close behind. She could hear him thrashing through the underbrush.

She shoved to her feet. In the shadows, she could barely make out a thicket of vines on her right. Without hesitation, she plunged into the clump of vegetation, pulled herself into a tight ball, hid her face in her hands and waited.

Breathing heavily, her pursuer raced past.

Jennifer waited and tried to ignore the vine scraping the back of her neck and the faint rustle in the leaves at her feet. If she thought too long about bugs, snakes and other critters that might be sharing the thicket with her, she'd scream.

A few minutes later, she heard Crutchfield backtrack on the trail, muttering to himself. The sound of his footsteps disappeared in the distance. Again, she waited, hoping he had returned to the inn, praying he hadn't recognized her.

After several long minutes, she lifted her head and listened. The surrounding woods were absolutely still. Convinced that Crutchfield had deserted the chase, she crawled from her hiding place, dusted leaves from her clothing and stood upright.

Out of nowhere, a figure loomed behind her and a strong hand closed over her mouth. Crutchfield had her. She almost fainted with fear.

"What the hell are you doing out here?" a familiar voice hissed in her ear.

Her knees buckled, and she would have fallen if Dylan hadn't caught her. He released her mouth, grabbed her roughly by the shoulders and turned her to face him.

"Well?" he demanded.

She raised her fist and pounded angrily on his chest. "You're doing it again!"

"Doing what?"

"Scaring me to death!"

"You deserve to be scared. Don't you have better sense that to crawl through a strange woods alone?"

"I wasn't alone. Crutchfield was after me."

"Not any more. I watched him go inside several minutes ago."

"How did you sneak up on me?" she demanded. "I didn't hear a thing."

"I grew up in the woods, remember? I learned how to move without tipping off my prey."

She realized then that she was wearing his jacket, and he was out in the frigid air in only his shirt-sleeves. She shrugged out of the jacket and handed it to him. "I was trying to search Crutchfield's car."

"For what?" He took the jacket without comment and pulled it on.

"For the gun that killed Max Thorne, for starters. I was hoping to find it in the glove compartment."

"And?"

"The car was locked. Then Crutchfield came outside to get something from the car and saw me. I ran."

"Did he recognize you?" He held her arm and led her along the path toward the parking lot.

"I doubt it. Not in the dark. Guess he thought I was just a common thief."

"Which is what you would have been if you'd taken anything from his vehicle."

"Now you're talking like a cop."

"I *am* a cop."

"And I'm just trying to save my life."

Dylan stopped on the path. "What do you think I'm trying to do, you little idiot?"

"Idiot?" She started to express her outrage at the term, but before she could say more, Dylan swept her into his arms and covered her mouth with his own. She forgot her anger, the seeping cold and Crutchfield. Her world contracted to one tiny spot of earth in a small woods, a world of warmth, safety and love. Returning his kiss, she stood on tiptoe and draped her arms around his neck. Nothing had ever felt so right as Dylan's arms, Dylan's lips, and this time, *he* had kissed her, of his own free will.

He lifted his head suddenly, and his breath came in short white puffs, visible in the cold night air. His eyes blazed dark, passion-filled. "What are we standing out here for? We have a perfectly good bed in that ridiculously overpriced room upstairs.''

Her heart hammered against her chest. Had he meant what she thought he did, or was he still suffering from exhaustion and longing only for sleep?

He laid his arm across her shoulders, and together they worked their way back along the woodsy path to the edge of the garden. As they stepped onto the brick walk that led to the rear entrance, Tom Putnam charged out the back door and approached them.

''Did you see him?'' their host asked.

''Who?'' Dylan said.

''The stranger Mr. O'Riley saw hanging around the parking lot. He chased the man into the woods, but couldn't catch him.''

''We haven't seen anyone,'' Jennifer said, ''and we even walked a ways into the woods. It's a beautiful night.''

Putnam stood beneath a lamppost, his usually genial expression replaced by concern. ''Maybe I should call the sheriff.''

''Was anything taken?'' Dylan asked.

Putnam shook his head. ''O'Riley thinks he ran the thief off before he could steal anything.''

''I'm a police officer,'' Dylan explained. ''I suggest you report what happened and ask the sheriff to have a deputy cruise the parking area a couple times tonight, just in case the thief returns.''

Putnam look relieved. ''Good idea. I'll give the sheriff a call right away. Thanks.''

He turned and hurried inside.

Jennifer nudged Dylan with her elbow. "There *was* no thief. Are you bending the truth again?"

Dylan was unapologetic. "Putnam will rest easier if he follows my suggestion. That's the least I can do after the worry you've caused him."

"*I* caused him? What about Crutchfield?"

Dylan fixed her with a look that made her insides melt. "Crutchfield isn't going anywhere tonight, and neither are we. Why don't we forget him until morning?"

She nodded, not daring to speak. Her heart was beating in her throat, and all she could think of was kissing Dylan again and how her body ached for him.

And of the big canopied bed awaiting them upstairs.

A few minutes later, Jennifer drew the curtains across the exposed bay window of their room, sealing them in an intimate cocoon of soft light, sweet fragrance and undisturbed quiet. Without speaking, Dylan pulled her into his arms and held her, cradling her against the wide expanse of his chest as if she were the most precious woman on earth.

Now was the time for confession. She had to let him know the truth before he made love to her, because, knowing Dylan and his strict moral code, that lovemaking would be a commitment, a solemn pledge between a man and a woman. No one-night stands for a man of Dylan's principles.

But the words caught in her throat, froze on her lips. How could she tell him now and break the spell that encircled them? She wanted to shut out the world, close out reality, deny what she'd done.

All she wanted was to love him.

Slowly, and with a reverence that brought tears to her eyes, he tugged her sweater over her head and undid the buttons of her blouse. With deft fingers, he finished undressing her, then scooped her in his arms and carried her to the wide bed. Giddiness enfolded her, watching him enjoying the sight of her. All her self-consciousness was lost in the love reflected in his eyes.

Without breaking the hold of his gaze, he kicked off his shoes, shed his clothes and lay beside her. He pulled her along the length of him, and she reveled in the sensation of her bare flesh against his. She surrendered with a sigh when he lowered his head and pressed his lips against her heart. His mouth caressed her breasts, and when he slid his fingers between her legs, agonizing pleasure detonated in every cell of her being.

He smiled at her delight, a slow, sexy smile that took away what little breath she had left. He kissed her again, a probing, demanding kiss that made her want him as she'd never wanted anything else in her life.

"Now," she begged.

Positioning himself above her, he tipped her hips to meet his thrust and pleasure cascaded through her until she gasped with excitement. She gripped his shoulders and gave herself to the primal rhythm that joined them into one inseparable being. With her gaze locked to his, she whirled into dizzying heights, until she plunged over the edge of reality into a glorious, star-studded oblivion, where nothing existed but the two of them.

"Jennifer," he cried at climax.

Like a frigid cascade, the name snapped her back to reality, and she feared what she had done.

SEVERAL MINUTES LATER, she sat in one end of an enormous claw-footed bathtub, up to her chin in hot water and bubbles. Dylan faced her at the other end of the tub.

"I could get used to this," he said.

"Bathing?" she teased.

"Making love with a beautiful woman and then sharing my bath with her." His eyes burned hot with desire and a deeper, purer emotion.

Her conscience pricked her and she changed the subject.

"Well, Dick Tracy, what do you suggest we do tomorrow?"

He flashed her a randy grin. "Stay in that big bed until checkout time."

She splashed water at him. "I mean what do we do about Crutchfield? We still need physical evidence before we go to the police."

Dylan picked up a fluffy washcloth and plunged it beneath the water. Picking up one of her feet, he began to scrub her toes. The sensation of his fingers kneading her foot made concentration difficult.

"Too bad the man is such a stickler for locks," Dylan said. "If we could search his house and office, I'm sure we'd find something to incriminate him."

"No lock is perfect," she hinted.

"I'm *not* breaking in," Dylan said. "We don't want to hamper anything we find with legal restrictions."

She smiled smugly. "You won't have to break in to his office. When I left his employment, I took my key. If he hasn't changed the locks—and he's too miserly to do that—we can just walk in and find what we need."

He kissed the sole of her foot. "Any other little tidbits of information you haven't told me?"

She drew a deep breath. The moment of truth had arrived.

Raising her head, she met his gaze head-on. "Just one."

He cocked an eyebrow. "What's that?"

"I'm *not* Jennifer Reid."

Chapter Ten

While Dylan sat in stunned silence, she stepped from the tub and wrapped a terry robe around herself.

He suddenly found his voice. "What do you mean, you're *not* Jennifer Reid?"

She jerked the robe's sash tightly around her waist. "Jennifer Reid is dead."

His mouth dropped open in horror. "You didn't—"

"No, I didn't kill her. She died in a train derailment."

Dylan stood and climbed out of the tub. His firm, tanned body glowed golden in the soft light, and the veins in his neck stood out in anger. "If you're not Jennifer Reid, who the hell are you?"

"It's—"

He grimaced and held up his hands. "Let me guess. It's a long story, right?"

"I was going to tell you earlier tonight. Honest. But then we got—sidetracked."

"Earlier tonight? How about several weeks ago? You lied to Miss Bessie about your identity, and you lied to me. What kind of woman are you?"

"Scared to death." She tilted her face to meet his gaze.

He looked achingly handsome, even with his face etched with indignation and his dark eyes flashing with anger. "This story about Crutchfield and Thorne's murder—did you make that up, too?"

She shook her head. "Everything I've told you about Crutchfield is true. I did work for him. But my name isn't Jennifer Reid. I'm Rachel O'Riley."

The name sounded foreign on her lips. She had posed as Jennifer for so long, she had begun to think of herself as Jennifer.

Dylan yanked on a robe, turned and stalked into the bedroom. She followed.

He stood before the fireplace, his back to her, hands gripping the edge of the mantel, and he didn't turn around when she sat in the chair beside the fire. He was shutting her out, just as she'd feared he would. She had offended his honor and his pride, and she doubted he'd ever forgive her.

"I'll tell you everything from the beginning—no more lies," she promised, "if you'll listen."

He sat in the chair across the hearth and fixed her with a laser-like stare. He would know if she lied. She had probably already spoiled all her chances with him, but she would try to redeem herself with the truth. She hated to think how she'd feel if the truth wasn't enough.

"My real name is Rachel O'Riley," she said. "I was born in Missouri and lived there on my parents' farm until just a few years ago. My parents both died shortly after catastrophic floods ruined their land. I left Missouri to attend college for a couple of years and returned after graduating with an associate degree as a paralegal.''

"Missouri's a long way from Atlanta," he said with the bluntness of a ruthless interrogator. "How did you end up there?"

"My college roommate was from Atlanta. When I visited her after graduation, I saw Crutchfield's ad for a paralegal. With my parents gone and the farm sold, I had nothing to hold me in Missouri. I applied for the job, and Crutchfield hired me."

"When?"

"Almost a year ago. But I knew as soon as I started working for him that I'd made a mistake. I couldn't stand the man."

"Why didn't you leave?"

"Holding my first job only a few months wouldn't look very good on my resumé. I decided to tough it out.

"About six months ago, I saw an ad in a national newspaper from a rancher in Montana. He was offering a business arrangement, a marriage in name only."

"Good God! Why would he do that?"

"He was a widower who needed someone to care for his young son, someone his son could call "Mom." But he wasn't ready for the emotional involvement of a real marriage. He promised not only regular pay but a portion of the ranch's profits. The marriage—and salary—would end when the boy graduated from high school."

"And you seriously considered this?" He looked at her as if she'd lost her mind.

She realized if she hadn't been desperate, she would never have considered the offer. "I was miserable at the law office. I had no close ties, no living relatives. Being part of a family again seemed an attractive idea at the time, so I corresponded with the man, Wade Garrett. Eventually I told him I'd come to Montana to meet him and his son Jordan before making a final decision."

Dylan shook his head in amazement. "This has to be the truth. Even *you* couldn't make up a story this crazy."

She winced at his oblique insult. "When I discovered that Crutchfield had killed Max Thorne, I knew I had to leave. Escaping to Montana seemed the perfect solution. I could hide on the Garrett ranch, and by marrying, I'd have a new identity."

"What changed your mind? Or did you just finally come to your senses?"

She flinched again at the sarcasm in his voice. "Crutchfield followed me. He caught up with me at the train station in Chicago, saw me through the window as the train was leaving the station. From his letters, I knew Wade Garrett was a good man. I couldn't place him and his son in danger from Crutchfield."

"How does Jennifer Reid work into this?"

She closed her eyes, remembering Crutchfield's face, contorted with anger when he spied her through the window of the departing train. "It started in Chicago."

Not leaving anything out, she told Dylan her story.

WITH A SIGH of relief, she had felt the train lurch forward and move slowly from the depot in Chicago. She had risked a peek from behind her paper and caught Crutchfield's malevolent gaze as he stared, rage coloring his face, at the departing train.

Her heart had thudded louder than the crescendo-ing clack of wheels against the rails. She wasn't out of the woods yet. If he'd recognized her, he could travel by car and be waiting at the next station.

She forced herself to breathe deeply. She couldn't think straight if she wasn't calm. If she could avoid Crutchfield until she reached her destination, she would have that new name, new home and safety at last. Surely those changes would throw him off her trail. The farther the train clicked along the tracks, the more optimistic she felt.

But her fear had returned with a vengeance at each stop, and she'd hidden in the rest room until the train started up again. Once it was rolling, she had care-fully searched the cars to make sure Crutchfield hadn't boarded. The train had sped through Wiscon-sin, Minnesota and North Dakota. By the time it en-tered eastern Montana with no sign of him, she was hoping she'd lost him.

But she knew from experience how persistent he would be.

He'd followed her all the way from Atlanta. Now he knew she was heading for the Northwest. Unless she changed her plans, it was only a matter of time before he tracked her down.

Her apprehension grew as the train passed through Glacier National Park. She tried to block her fears by striking up a conversation with her seatmate, Jennifer Reid, a woman about her own age, who was on her way to Seattle.

"I'm a widow," the blond-haired, green-eyed woman explained. "My parents died when I was young, and I have no other relatives. After an unhappy marriage, I've decided it's time to start a new life and leave my past behind."

An orphan herself with no living relatives, Rachel felt an immediate affinity to the woman. They chatted for a long time, experiencing the freedom that comes from conversing with a stranger you know you'll never see again. Rachel didn't tell her seatmate, however, about the man who stalked her. For a few blessed hours, she managed to push Larry Crutchfield from her mind.

A sudden jolt interrupted their conversation.

With a swiftness that sucked the oxygen from her lungs, the railroad car jumped the tracks. It lurched sideways and jackknifed away from the steep mountainside. She watched in horror as thick timbers that supported snowsheds above the tracks snapped like toothpicks. The car barreled through the timber barricade and slid toward a deep ravine.

Flung like a rag doll by the careening coach, she smacked hard against the armrest. She winced in pain as her ribs cracked.

The car upended.

She grabbed in vain at something, anything, to

keep from bouncing like a sock tumbling in a dryer, and caught hold of the back of a seat.

The toppling car churned with tossed bodies and flying luggage. A hard-sided suitcase collided with her shoulder blades and rebounded into the chaos.

''Help!'' her seatmate cried and lunged against Rachel, seizing her arm in a viselike grip. The woman's panicked shriek blended with the terrified screams of other passengers.

Acrid smoke filled the air, blinding Rachel as the car shifted again. The derailed train gathered speed and plunged unchecked into the mountain gorge.

With her seatmate's wail reverberating in her ear, Rachel pitched against a window. Flames erupted a few feet away and blasted her with a wave of searing heat.

Oh, God, they were going to be burned alive!

The real Jennifer had released the grip on her arm, and Rachel glanced down to see the woman unconscious on the floor, blood seeping from a wound on the back of her head. She slapped the woman gently on her cheeks, trying to rouse her, but without effect. Grabbing up both their backpacks, she dragged the injured woman toward the entrance, barely managing to keep a few feet ahead of the flames licking their way up the aisle of the car.

Other passengers battered past them, shoving and screaming, but no one stopped to help. Rachel knew she could move faster and would have a better chance of saving herself if she deserted Jennifer, but she also knew that leaving the woman would condemn her to a horrible, fiery death.

Eyes and lungs burning with smoke, her arms and back aching from strain, Rachel tugged the dead weight of her dazed companion toward the exit, its glowing red sign barely visible through the haze. When she reached the door, she saw with horror that this end of the car was elevated. It was a good six-foot jump to the ground.

Suddenly arms reached up out of the smoke to help her, and a conductor with a torn uniform and soot-grimed face received Jennifer's limp body as Rachel eased it out the door. Still holding both backpacks, she leaped from the car, her speedy exit hastened by the flames at her back.

She followed the conductor who carried Jennifer to a level spot on the rock-strewn floor of the gorge, a safe distance from the burning train. The roar of a river swollen with melted snow sounded nearby. The conductor laid Jennifer on the ground and felt for a pulse.

"Is she okay?" Rachel asked.

He shook his head sadly. "I don't think she made it."

Rachel felt a sharp pang of loss.

The conductor peered at Rachel through the haze. "You hurt? A doctor and nurse among the passengers have set up a triage station a little ways down the gorge. Medical teams—and the damned media—will be flying in by the dozens."

"I'll be okay. I just want to sit here a while with my friend."

He nodded grimly and hurried away to help someone else.

Rachel glanced at the woman stretched on the ground beneath the gigantic evergreens and experienced a wave of deep sorrow. Jennifer had seemed so excited about starting her new life, and now all her expectations had been canceled in an instant.

The way Rachel's life would be if Crutchfield caught up with her.

The conductor's parting words came back to her. The media were on the scene, and soon the spectacular crash would be broadcast over every television station in the country.

He would be watching.

She had to hide. She had to retrace her steps in the opposite direction, leave the Northwest and throw him off her trail.

But first she removed her jacket and gently covered Jennifer's face. Kneeling beside the body, Rachel issued up a fervent prayer for the woman's soul. In that instant, like a divine message, a solution to her own dilemma occurred to her.

Scrambling quickly before anyone else approached, she removed her identification and the address where she was headed in Montana from her backpack and placed them in Jennifer's bag.

Jennifer was close to Rachel's height and weight, and her eyes were also green, although her blond hair lacked Rachel's fiery red tones. With the switched identification papers, Jennifer would be identified as Rachel O'Riley. When the obituary hit the national papers, Crutchfield, thinking his goal of killing Rachel had been achieved by the train wreck, would abandon his pursuit.

She glanced quickly into the dead woman's backpack and removed all Jennifer's papers and any form of identification. Among them she found a Tennessee driver's license.

Rachel's new name would be Jennifer Reid.

She stuffed the dead woman's license and other papers into her backpack and hoisted it onto her aching shoulder. After tying a scarf to hide her red-hued hair and covering her eyes with sunglasses, she had made her way down the gorge, away from the crowd gathering around the wreckage.

"IN WHITEFISH, I caught a bus and headed for Tennessee," she told Dylan. "If I was going to become Jennifer Reid, I had to learn all I could about her. I spent a week researching in the Memphis library. My paralegal skills helped me discover all I needed to know, including the fact that Jennifer had no living relatives.

"Once I had enough information, I moved on to Nashville and took the waitress job at the resort, just like I told you."

"And you left Nashville when Michael Johnson showed up asking questions?"

She nodded. "I remembered Jennifer telling me on the train about her childhood visits to Casey's Cove and how secluded it is. I decided it would be a perfect place to hide. I went to Asheville first, and that's where I saw Miss Bessie's ad in the paper. It seemed like an answer to a prayer. I had no idea how good Crutchfield's hit man would be at tracking me down."

"Why didn't you tell me the truth when we met? I would have tried to help you." His iron demeanor cracked, and she glimpsed regret in his eyes.

"I didn't know Johnson was still on my trail. And I didn't know that I'd be falling in love with you," she added, her voice heavy with sadness, her eyes filled with tears.

Dylan sat staring silently at the dwindling flames licking the embers in the fireplace. His expression was neutral, and she feared his feelings for her had burned into ashes like the ones he studied so intently.

"You stole another woman's identity," he said finally.

She nodded. "Are you going to arrest me?"

"Did you access her bank accounts, use her credit cards?"

"No! What do you think am I?"

At the look he shot her, she wished she could grab back the question. He obviously considered her a thief. And a liar. And maybe even worse.

"Jennifer..." he paused, "...what am I supposed to call you?"

She shrugged. What he called her didn't matter anymore, not when his feelings toward her were so negative. "I'm used to Jennifer."

He nodded. "It's late. You'd better get some sleep."

"In a while. I'm too keyed up to sleep now."

He stood. "I'm going to bed."

"Goodnight," she whispered, wishing circumstances were different, that she could climb into bed and fall asleep in his arms. With his present attitude, lying next to him would be like sleeping with a glacier.

She focused on the fire, but she heard him drop the terry robe, and in her imagination, she could see his magnificent body, lean from exercise and golden from the sun, as he slid beneath the covers. Just a short time ago, they had made passionate love in that bed, and she'd experienced the greatest happiness of her life.

But she'd gone from ecstasy to agony in less than sixty minutes.

She waited until his even breathing indicated he'd fallen asleep. Careful not to waken him, she lifted a folded blanket from the foot of the bed, draped it around herself, and lay down on the cushioned window seat. Closing her eyes, she prayed sleep would come quickly and put her out of her misery.

DYLAN WAKENED with a start and sat upright in bed. For a moment, he couldn't remember his surroundings, but as his eyes adjusted to the dimness, he realized where he was. The luminous face of his watch indicated he'd overslept. It was almost nine o'clock.

A glance at the other side of the bed revealed it empty, unslept in, and his gaze scanned the room until it lit on Jennifer, curled beneath a blanket on the window seat, her blond hair spread like sunshine on a quilted pillow. A pleasing warmth spread through him as he remembered their lovemaking the previous night, but it quickly dissipated as the memory of her confession surfaced.

Jennifer wasn't Jennifer at all, but a fraud and a

thief. He should never have allowed himself to care for her, but he hadn't been able to keep himself from it.

Earlier last night when he had first awakened and found her gone, he'd guessed immediately what she was up to. He'd tiptoed down the hall toward Crutchfield's room to find her and had been surprised by Crutchfield coming out his door.

"I'm going down to the car for that present I bought you," the attorney had called to Elissa before shutting the door.

Dylan had ducked into the alcove that housed the ice machine until the attorney had passed, then tailed him down the stairs to the rear entrance. Dylan's heart had stuck in his throat when he glimpsed Jennifer plowing through the hedge on the other side of Crutchfield's Mercedes. When the attorney spotted her and gave chase, Dylan had followed, fearful of what Crutchfield might do if he caught her.

But Jennifer had been as facile at hiding as she had been at dodging the truth. She'd managed to conceal herself in a thicket until Crutchfield gave up his search. Dylan had hidden as well until the attorney returned to the inn. When Jennifer had emerged from her hiding place and he'd grabbed her, the look of stark terror on her face had stirred his emotions. Giddy with relief that she was unharmed, he'd kissed her.

That had been his first mistake.

Making love to her had been his second.

He had hoped eventually to turn Crutchfield over to the cops and take Jennifer back to Casey's Cove with him. He'd even toyed with the idea of marrying her. But now his mother's words came back to haunt him. He'd asked her once several years ago how she and his father had maintained such a long, happy union.

"We love each other," she'd answered simply. His mother had never been a complicated woman.

"But there has to be more than that," he'd argued.

He could see her now, gray hair cut short and stylish, her lined face smiling, hazel eyes twinkling. "You're right. There is more. For one, your father is my best friend. Always has been."

That fact was no news to Dylan. All his life he had witnessed how much they enjoyed each other's company.

"And second and probably the most important," she'd added, "is that we trust each other. Love can't grow without trust. It withers and dies like a flower without water."

Gazing at Jennifer's pretty face, relaxed and innocent in sleep, Dylan realized any chance of a life with her was doomed. How could he trust such a perpetual liar?

Turning his back on her, he dressed and went downstairs for breakfast. He'd have to bring Jennifer's meal back on a tray, since she couldn't risk being seen by Crutchfield. The sooner Dylan could leave this place the better, especially the room upstairs with its memories of lovemaking in that huge bed, memories that curdled now like sour milk when he recalled them.

Tom Putnam was at the front desk when Dylan descended the stairs.

"Sleep well?" his host asked.

Dylan nodded. "But Jennifer's a bit under the weather this morning."

The picture of discretion, Putnam made no comment. He merely gestured toward the room opposite the main parlor. "Breakfast is being served. If you like, we'll send up a tray again for your wife."

Dylan didn't correct his host. "Thanks."

When he entered the dining room, he found several guests seated around a huge mahogany table. Breakfast was spread buffet style on the matching sideboard. He helped himself to grits, ham, red-eye gravy and scrambled eggs and purposely took the seat opposite Crutchfield and Mrs. Thorne.

"Good morning," he said.

Mrs. Thorne nodded coolly and Crutchfield acknowledged his greeting abruptly before returning his attention to his overloaded plate.

Dylan studied the man. He didn't need Jennifer's remembrances to pick up on the attorney's coldness. He had seen for himself the ice in the man's blue eyes.

"Hear you had some trouble in the parking lot last night," Dylan said.

Crutchfield jerked his head up. "How did you know?"

"I'd stepped out for a breath of air and ran into our host. He said someone had tried to break into your car. Anything stolen?"

"What business is it of yours?" Crutchfield's tone matched the coldness in his eyes.

"Well, first, I have a vehicle parked out there, too, and second, I'm a police officer. Crime is always my business."

Crutchfield scrutinized him with a look that would have made a lesser man cower, but he didn't frighten Dylan. Although Jennifer had lied to Dylan about many things, she had her former boss pegged. He was disagreeable, arrogant and conceited.

But was he a murderer?

Tom Putnam appeared at Dylan's elbow and filled his coffee cup from a silver pot. "Sheriff's deputy checked things out last night. Found where someone entered the trees from the parking lot, but he lost the trail. He guesses the would-be thief fled through the woods to the main road. Must have had a car waiting."

"What if he comes back?" Crutchfield demanded. "I don't want my car broken into or vandalized."

"I'm hiring a security service today," Putnam announced. "A guard will patrol the parking lot at night from now on."

Dylan would have felt guilty for his part in the deception, but he knew at Putnam's exorbitant rates, he could well afford to pay the security team.

"You from around here?" Dylan asked Crutchfield.

"Savannah." The attorney lied with even more ease than Jennifer. "And you?"

"North Carolina," Dylan said. "Just passing through."

Mrs. Thorne leaned toward Crutchfield and whispered in his ear. The attorney scowled, threw his napkin on the table and stood. He pulled out the woman's chair, and the two left the room without a word to any of the other guests.

Dylan finished his breakfast in silence.

Kyra brought a tray, and he helped her select fresh fruit, pastries and coffee, then carried the tray upstairs.

When he opened the door to the room, Jennifer was dressed and seated in the chair by the fire. Her eyes widened in surprise when she saw him.

"I thought you'd gone," she said.

"Gone?" He set her breakfast on the table by her chair and tried to keep his traitorous heart from sympathizing with her.

"Back to North Carolina. I wouldn't blame you."

"I'll take you back to Atlanta after breakfast."

He crossed to the window and stood staring out at the autumn leaves glistening in the morning sun.

"You don't believe me, do you?" Only the tiniest tremor in her voice gave away her distress.

"That you're not Jennifer Reid?"

"No, that Crutchfield is a murderer."

He shrugged. This morning he was having a hard time sorting out exactly what his beliefs and feelings were.

"I'd swear that what I've told you is true," she said, "but I suppose a liar's word doesn't carry much weight."

"Eat your breakfast," he said without turning. "We should get on the road soon."

He heard the clatter of a cup against a saucer, but he continued to avoid looking at Jennifer. The sight of her softened his heart, and he needed to make his decisions with a cool, clear mind.

Images of the attorney at breakfast tumbled through his head. Larry Crutchfield was a despicable man, but was he a murderer?

And did Dylan want to hang around Jennifer and Atlanta long enough to find out?

Chapter Eleven

Fighting against a sadness that threatened to crush her, Jennifer shoved away her untouched breakfast tray and stood. "I'm ready to leave if you are."

Dylan turned from the window and nodded, avoiding her eyes. "Better wear dark glasses in case we run into Crutchfield in the hall."

With a heavy heart, she gathered her belongings, slipped on her sunglasses, and took one last glance at the room where so much had happened, where her life had gone from bliss to nightmare. Thankful to place the scene behind her, she opened the door and stepped into the hall.

Without a word, Dylan followed, and together they descended the stairs.

At the front desk, Dylan checked out with Tom Putnam.

"Hope you folks enjoyed your stay," the genial host said as they turned to leave. "And hope you're feeling better, Mrs. Blackburn."

Mrs. Blackburn.

Jennifer flashed the innkeeper a smile that was more of a grimace. That was the only time she'd ever be called Mrs. Blackburn. It'd be a cold day in hell before Dylan ever trusted her again, much less asked her to marry him.

The ride back to Atlanta was quiet and strained. The atmosphere in the truck cab was so tense, Jennifer couldn't wait to get out when Dylan pulled to the curb in front of her apartment.

"Thanks for bringing me back. I'd say I'm sorry again, but I know you believe sorry isn't enough." She headed for the outside stairway.

At the sound of a door slamming behind her, she turned. Dylan was following her up the walk.

"Where are you going?" she asked.

"With you." His expression was stern, and she'd have given what little of her savings she had left to see him smile again.

Recalling that he'd left his travel kit and backpack in her apartment, she reckoned he'd hit the road as soon as he'd gathered his belongings.

Once inside, however, he settled in a chair and made no move to collect his things.

Puzzled, she perched on the sofa across from him. "Okay, I give up."

He wrinkled his brow. "Give up?"

"I'm no mind reader. Maybe you can fill me in on what you intend to do."

He nodded solemnly. "On the ride back, I gave this whole situation a lot of thought."

"Which situation?" She dared hope he was talking about the two of them.

"The Max Thorne murder."

She hid her disappointment. "And what conclusion did you come to?"

"I could go back to Casey's Cove and leave you to fend for yourself."

Her heart sank at the thought of his leaving.

"But if you're right," he continued, "and Crutchfield's the murderer, I'd be shirking my duty if I don't try to make him answer for his crime."

"I *am* right. If it takes a lie-detector test, I'll prove that to you."

"And if I returned home and something happened to you—"

She studied his expression, searching in vain for a sign of the caring that he'd shown last night.

"—I'd feel guilty as hell."

"Guilty?" Was that all? Not sad or sorry, just responsible?

If he'd noted her dismayed reaction, he didn't show it. "So I've decided to stay and search Crutchfield's office."

Anger got the better of her. He didn't believe her, but he'd stay to help just to assuage his conscience.

"I can inspect the office myself," she insisted hotly, "and you can go back to Casey's Cove with a clear conscience and forget about me. I don't intend to let Crutchfield or Michael Johnson get their hands on me."

"You can't guarantee that," he said evenly, obviously unperturbed by her heated outburst.

"Neither can you," she shot back. "I've stayed out of their clutches for the last five months. I can survive a little longer. At least long enough to prove Larry Crutchfield murdered Max Thorne.''

The corners of his lips lifted in a ghost of a smile. ''I have to give you credit, Jennifer-Rachel. You have more courage than most men I know.''

''Don't kid yourself. This isn't courage. It's sheer desperation. I want my life back, and putting Crutchfield behind bars is the only way to do it.''

He pushed to his feet. ''Then we'd better get busy. We're wasting time talking. While Crutchfield's still in Madison is the perfect opportunity to search his office. Unless he has partners or associates who work on Saturdays?''

She shook her head. ''He's a one-man law firm. He's so arrogant, no one else could stand working with him for very long.''

He started for the door and turned to her. ''You have the key?''

She patted her purse.

''Then let's go.'' He opened the door and waved her through.

FOLLOWING Jennifer's directions, Dylan navigated through the light Saturday traffic of Atlanta's Buckhead district. He was glad he didn't have to concentrate too heavily on his driving. The debate waging inside demanded all his attention.

Part of him wanted nothing more than to love, cherish and protect the woman beside him for the rest of his life. But his more rational side rebelled, insisting that Rachel O'Riley, alias Jennifer Reid, with her regrettable propensity for distorting the truth, would make his life a long, bumpy road of distrust and uncertainties.

The harder he tried to stop thinking about it, the more he recalled the memory of her in his arms last night and the love shining in her eyes—before she'd dropped the bombshell of her false identity. Despite her flaws, no woman had even fascinated, excited or captivated him as she had. She had intelligence and good humor in abundance. She was definitely no quitter. *Feisty* described her to a T. A lesser woman would have cracked under the strain of the past five months.

And he couldn't deny that she loved people. He'd seen her interact with Miss Bessie, Raylene and Sissy and too many other residents of Casey's Cove to count, had seen them respond to her warmth and friendliness. Surely a woman with that much affection in her couldn't be all bad.

But could he spend a lifetime with a woman he couldn't trust?

What he needed was distance and time to sort out his feelings, heal his disappointment and decide whether to keep Jennifer in his life. But he couldn't leave her now, not until he was sure she was safe. *To serve and protect* was more than a motto for him. It was his reason for living.

"Headache?" Jennifer broke into his thoughts. "I have some aspirin in my purse."

"No, thanks." It would take more than a few pills to cure what ailed him. He put on his sunglasses and worked to smooth the scowl that had prompted her concern.

"Turn left here," she instructed when they reached a modern steel-and-glass office building. "There's a parking garage below."

Minutes later they stepped from the elevator into the third-floor corridor and crossed the hall to an impressive double door marked in brass letters, Lawrence A. Crutchfield, Attorney at Law. Jennifer searched her purse for her keys, then unlocked the door. Dylan followed her inside to the elegant reception area, an interior decorator's creation of glass and brass, burgundy and hunter's green. Crutchfield's clients must be extremely wealthy, he noted.

At least until they received his bill.

"I never thought I'd come here again." She glanced around and shivered, as if haunted by bad memories. "Where do you want to start?"

"Can you locate Max Thorne's file? It might hold some clues."

"This way." She turned right down a wide corridor and paused at the first door. "This was my office. Crutchfield's is next. Wait there and I'll bring you Thorne's records from the file room."

Dylan entered Larry Crutchfield's office and looked around. The spacious corner room featured floor-to-ceiling windows on two sides. The other walls were wood-paneled, covered with memorabilia and pictures of Crutchfield with various celebrities, including presidents and media moguls.

Jennifer was right about the attorney's friends in high places, Dylan thought. No wonder she'd been reluctant to blow the whistle on the murder. Without solid proof, no one would have believed her.

In addition to the celebrity photographs, various golf and tennis trophies and a huge gold-framed mirror completed the collection on the wall. The mirror hung exactly opposite the massive desk, where the egocentric Crutchfield could bask in his own reflection.

Searching the office took only a few minutes. He found no sign of a gun in the desk drawers, the credenza behind the desk, or even in the adjoining bathroom, accessed through a door in one of the paneled walls. He returned to the office and checked behind the photographs for a wall safe.

Nothing.

Turning back the carpet in each corner of the room, he searched for a floor safe.

Again, nothing.

Moving behind the massive desk, he eyed the crime scene. Had Thorne been seated in either of the two club chairs in front of the desk, he would have been an easy target. Dylan inspected the leather of the chairs for signs of bullet holes or visible repairs but found none. Maybe Thorne had lunged for Crutchfield across his desk when the attorney plugged him.

Dylan glanced at the tall windows and frowned. Jennifer had said the murder occurred at night, but there were no blinds or draperies on the windows. Surely the man hadn't committed murder where anyone passing on the street could have witnessed it?

"Problem?" Jennifer came in and placed a thick file on the desk in front of him.

"No blinds. If Crutchfield shot Thorne at night

with the lights on, he might as well have been on stage. There's constant traffic out there on the boulevard.''

Jennifer smiled, circled the desk, and leaned over him to reach beneath the surface. Her honeysuckle scent sent a wave of longing shuddering through him, and he had to force himself not to reach for her.

She flicked a switch beneath the desk and stepped back. Instantly the clear glass of the windows changed to an opaque hue.

''State of the art,'' she said. ''Crutchfield spared no expense for his own convenience. My former office, however, has mini-blinds.''

''Better turn these back to clear,'' he suggested. ''No need to call attention to ourselves.''

She hit the switch again and moved toward the door. ''I'll be in the library, going through financial records on the computer.''

He opened the thick file and began to plow through the dry, legal language of contracts between Thorne's international delivery service and the businesses it served. After thirty minutes, he stood, stretched, and rubbed his bleary eyes.

''Thought you'd need this.'' Jennifer stood in the doorway with a steaming cup of coffee. He could sniff its tantalizing aroma all the way across the room.

He accepted the mug and half-emptied it in one swallow. ''Thanks.''

''Any luck?''

He shook his head. ''I'm no lawyer, but everything I've read seems on the up and up.''

Suddenly she froze and pressed a finger to her lips. The hall door lock clicked. Someone had opened it and entered the reception area of the office.

He flipped the Thorne file closed, rose from the desk and grabbed Jennifer by the arm. Opening the door in the paneling, he tugged her behind him into the adjoining bathroom. After closing the door soundlessly, he indicated the shower cubicle. Jennifer stepped inside. Dylan followed and drew the shower curtain to conceal them.

He held his breath and waited. He realized too late that he'd left the file on Crutchfield's desk, and he couldn't retrieve it without the risk of being seen by whoever had arrived at the law offices.

Jennifer gazed up at him, her remarkable green eyes round with alarm. He shot her a reassuring smile, pulled her close, and kept his arms around her. If Crutchfield had returned to find them, the attorney would have to go through him first if he tried to harm Jennifer.

She buried her head against his chest, and her soft hair tickled his nose. He could feel her heart pounding and the quickness of her breathing. She stiffened when a voice called out in the attorney's office.

"Mr. Crutchfield? Are you here?"

The unseen female rapped on the bathroom door. "Mr. Crutchfield?"

From her manner of address, Dylan guessed the woman was one of Crutchfield's employees. He only hoped she hadn't arrived to spend her entire Saturday afternoon catching up on work.

The woman didn't open the bathroom door, and Dylan waited for her to leave the adjoining office.

Meanwhile, the longer he held Jennifer, the more he wanted to kiss her, but he'd already promised himself distance in order to analyze his feelings. With her soft curves pressed against him, however, his rebellious body made its own decision. He hoped she wouldn't notice.

After waiting what seemed hours of agonizing pleasure, but was actually less than five minutes, Dylan released Jennifer and motioned for her to remain hidden in the shower. He crept to the door and opened it a tiny crack.

The office was empty.

Dylan eased out of the bathroom, moved quietly to the hall doorway, and listened. No sounds other than the muted hiss of the central heating system were evident. He quickly checked the rest of the rooms, but whoever had been there earlier had left. But had she noted the files out of place, the freshly made coffee, the lighted monitor in the library and reported them to security?

He returned to Jennifer in Crutchfield's office. "We'd better get out of here fast while the coast is clear."

Cheeks flushing an alluring pink from their close encounter, she nodded. "Let me get something first."

She sprinted down the corridor into the library. When she met him again seconds later, she was folding a printed sheet of paper and slipping it into her pocket. Outside the office, she relocked the door, and they entered the elevator without being seen.

They had just turned onto the boulevard from the office complex when a police car, lights flashing, crested the hill and headed toward them. The cruiser passed them and screeched into the complex. Once it had disappeared into the underground parking garage, Dylan pressed the accelerator.

"That was close," he said. "Our unexpected visitor must have called the cops."

"Just keep straight ahead," Jennifer said. "I'll tell you where to turn."

Euphoric over escaping their close call, he couldn't help grinning at her. "Mind telling me where we're going?"

She removed the folded paper from her pocket. "Lenny's Carpet Mart."

He nodded toward the printout. "What did you find?"

Her smile was triumphant. "A payment to Lenny's Carpet Mart made the day after Max Thorne was murdered."

"Don't get your hopes up. There's not much chance of finding Crutchfield's original carpet now. It's probably buried under tons of garbage in a landfill somewhere."

"We won't know till we try."

He found her optimism contagious but wondered at its source. For a woman with no family and a killer on her trail, she displayed an amazingly resilient spirit. He doubted he could show such optimism in her situation.

Ten minutes later, at her direction, he turned the truck into the parking lot of a strip-store shopping center. Lenny's Carpet Mart occupied the space on the far end of the building, a structure and location that had obviously seen better days.

They entered the carpet store, and Dylan's nose stung from the off-gases of racks of carpet samples and several layers of dust. A middle-aged woman with stringy hair, tired eyes and a Yorkshire terrier tucked in the crook of her arm approached them.

"Can I help you folks?" Her voice was pleasant, but the dog snarled, baring yellow teeth.

"We're looking for Lenny," Dylan said.

The woman calmed the dog and grinned. "You're looking at her. Name's Leonora, Lenny for short. What can I do for you?"

Jennifer stepped forward and without hesitation patted the scruffy dog. The animal relaxed, then preened under her attention.

"We're trying to trace a carpet," Jennifer explained.

She gave the woman the date Lenny's had installed new carpet in the law office and asked where she might find the carpet they'd removed.

Lenny narrowed her eyes and viewed Jennifer with suspicion. "Why would you want carpet that's probably been garbage for five months?"

Dylan started to explain, but Jennifer jumped in with her own story.

"You know how we women are," Jennifer said in a conspiratorial voice. "I'm buying new carpet for my living room, and when I worked for Mr. Crutchfield, I always *adored* the style and color he had in his office. If I could find that carpet and match it, I'm sure it would be perfect."

Lenny still looked skeptical, but Dylan could almost see the dollar signs flashing in her eyes. He was sure the carpet in Crutchfield's office hadn't been cheap and that Lenny was contemplating a sale.

"Just a minute." Lenny walked behind a sales counter, placed the dog in a large padded basket on the chipped Formica surface and pulled out a ledger. Flipping back a few pages, she stopped and poked her thin finger at the page. "Hank Bainbridge."

"Who's that?" Dylan asked.

"The man who installed Mr. Crutchfield's new carpet. He can tell you what he did with the old one." Lenny grabbed a pencil and a scrap of paper and scribbled an address. "He lives out in the country a good forty-five-minute drive from here."

Dylan took the paper and thanked her. Back in the truck, he handed the address to Jennifer. "Know where this is?"

Jennifer nodded and gave him directions.

HANK BAINBRIDGE'S trailer sat in a grove of slash pines several hundred feet off the highway. A pack of mongrel dogs apparently lived underneath it, because when Dylan's truck approached the yard, teeth bared and voices wailing, they surged from under the trailer and surrounded the vehicle.

A thin man with graying hair appeared at the door and hollered at the animals, who slunk back beneath the structure at his command.

Jennifer rolled down her window. "Mr. Bainbridge?"

"Who wants to know?" the man replied in a Southern drawl heavy with suspicion.

"Leonora—Lenny sent us," she explained. "We have some questions about a carpet."

Shrugging into a denim jacket that matched his faded overalls, the man left the trailer and approached the truck. "I'm Hank Bainbridge. You need a carpet installed?"

Jennifer shook her head. "I'm Jennifer Reid and this is Dylan Blackburn. He's a police officer and we're looking for a carpet you removed from an office building. It could be evidence in a crime."

Hank folded his arms on the window frame. "Sorry to disappoint you, but I take all the old carpets to the county landfill. They burn 'em in their incinerator."

"Oh, no." Jennifer slumped in her seat and watched her last chance at convicting Crutchfield evaporate into thin air.

Dylan leaned toward Hank. "Don't you ever make exceptions? Give a barely used carpet to a friend for use in his own home?"

Hank shuffled his feet and avoided their eyes. "Lenny says I'm to burn 'em all. She claims if I give away free carpet, it hurts her business."

Jennifer felt a spark of hope. "We're not looking to get you in trouble with your boss. We just need that carpet. It was removed from Larry Crutchfield's law office last May. A man was murdered there."

Hank groaned and rolled his eyes. "I told Ellie we shouldn't have kept it."

"You *have* the carpet?" Dylan asked.

Shamefaced, Hank nodded.

"All of it?" Jennifer asked.

"That was a big office," Hank said. "Except for the stain, the rug's like new, and there was enough to carpet our whole place."

"So you have it all?" Jennifer couldn't contain her excitement. "That's wonderful!"

"Wonderful for you, maybe," Hank grumbled. "What's Ellie going to do when she finds her carpet gone?"

"We don't need all of it," Dylan explained. "Just the part that has the stain. And we'll need you to sign an affidavit that it's the carpet you removed from the law office on that date."

Hank looked relieved. "That's no problem. I used the stained part in the floor of the closet. If I can find a close match, Ellie won't even miss it. I'll get it for you."

Minutes later, they were headed back to Atlanta with the infamous carpet, wrapped carefully in plastic, jammed between them.

"What if the crime lab doesn't find any blood?" she asked. "It looks like it's been scrubbed clean."

Dylan stared at the road ahead, keeping the emotional distance he'd established when he'd learned her true identity. When he spoke, his tone was professional, detached, and she ached at the loss of the intimacy they'd shared.

"You'd be surprised at how little forensics needs for a sample. I'm betting there's enough blood left to prove it's Max Thorne's."

Jennifer didn't know whether to laugh or cry. With luck, Crutchfield would soon be in jail and her life would be safe again. But Crutchfield's arrest would also mean Dylan, his duty to protect her fulfilled, would walk out of her life and return to Casey's Cove without her.

EARLY THAT evening, Dylan sat in the office of Atlanta detective Skip Hawkins. The setting sun threw golden rays across the desk cluttered with file folders and empty coffee cups where Hawkins sat, taking notes, while Jennifer told her story of the night Max Thorne was murdered.

Despite Dylan's attempts to distance himself from her, as he watched her give her clear, concise and fearless account of Crutchfield's crime he couldn't help admiring Jennifer's courage. She'd been as tenacious as a terrier on the attorney's trail, and if the lab reports produced the needed blood sample, thanks to her, her former boss would soon be behind bars. Jennifer would then be free to assume her true identity, to live her life without hiding, without fear.

Without him?

Dylan wanted to love her, he couldn't deny it. But how much good was love without trust? It would be a cold day in July before he could trust her after the lies she'd told him, and it wouldn't be fair to ask her to hang around long enough for him to see if he could rebuild that trust.

The ring of a phone on Hawkins's desk interrupted Dylan's thoughts. The detective picked up the receiver before it could ring again.

"Hawkins here." The man's blue eyes, looking as if they'd seen more trouble than any human should have to, narrowed, and his forehead furrowed beneath his sandy crew cut as he listened to the person on the other end of the line.

"Thanks." He slammed the phone into its cradle and turned to Jennifer. "The lab report supports your story."

Dylan breathed a sigh of relief. This time Jennifer's story had been right on the money. Guilt pricked him as he realized he'd had latent doubts about her truthfulness.

"The DNA matches Thorne?" she asked.

Hawkins shook his head. "DNA testing will take a while, but the blood type from the carpet matches Thorne's. It's here in his autopsy report. With your testimony, Bainbridge's affidavit that the carpet came from Crutchfield's office and the blood match, I can get a warrant to arrest Crutchfield and to search his home for a weapon. We'll pick him up as soon as he returns to Atlanta from Madison."

"He'll stay locked up until his trial?" she asked.

"No bail for a murder charge," Dylan explained. "You're safe now."

Her shoulders slumped with relief, and for the first time, her vulnerability was evident. More than anything, Dylan wanted to put his arms around her and hold her close, but his hesitation about trusting her kept him from comforting her.

"Will you need anything else from me before Crutchfield goes to court?" Jennifer asked Hawkins.

"I have your statement," the detective said, "but you will have to testify at the trial. That could be several months or more away. Better give me your address so I can get in touch with you."

Jennifer hesitated and cast Dylan a look he couldn't read. "I'm not sure where I'll be. I've been on the run so long, I don't have a permanent address. My apartment's only temporary. Can I let you know once I'm settled?"

"Sure." Hawkins stood and held out his hand. "I

appreciate what you've done, Miss O'Riley. It took a lot of guts."

She blushed an attractive tinge of pink, and Dylan felt desire stir within him.

"Not guts," she said. "Just desperation. I'm glad I can quit looking over my shoulder now."

"Thanks for your help, too." Hawkins shook Dylan's hand. "Miss O'Riley was lucky to have your protection."

"I was glad to help," Dylan said, "but Miss O'Riley is quite adept at taking care of herself."

Hawkins walked them to the door and waited as they entered the elevator and the door closed.

"Where to now?" Dylan wanted her to return to Casey's Cove with him, but he couldn't ask without implying more to their relationship than he was ready to admit.

"Back to the apartment." She stared at the control panel, avoiding his eyes. "You'll want to pick up your things before you head back to the mountains."

"Right."

Disappointment surged through him. He had hoped she'd return to Miss Bessie's, but she'd had a life in Atlanta before she arrived in Casey's Cove. It made sense that she might wish to pick up where she'd left off before Crutchfield came after her.

Neither of them spoke during the ride to her apartment. He followed her into the living room and began gathering his belongings. Torn between not wanting to leave her and fear of committing to a relationship doomed by mistrust, he dreaded saying goodbye. This might be the last time he'd see her.

"Can I ask you a favor?" she said.

"Sure."

"Promise you won't say yes unless you really mean it?"

She had piqued his curiosity. "I promise."

"Are you in a hurry?"

If she only knew how reluctant he was to leave. "Not especially. I'm not due back at work till Monday."

She drew a deep breath, like someone ready to plunge off a cliff. "I'm going to call Miss Bessie and ask if she'll have me back. If she agrees, can I catch a ride with you?"

He made himself pause, not to appear too eager. "Why not? I have room."

"Thank you." She turned, picked up the phone and punched in a number.

Dylan paced back and forth while the phone rang.

"Miss Bessie? This is Jennifer."

She paused, and Dylan could picture Miss Bessie on the other end of the line. What he couldn't guess was whether the old woman was glad to hear from her employee or angry at Jennifer's desertion.

"Yes, I'm fine," Jennifer said. "I'm sorry for the worry I've caused, Miss Bessie, and I'm hoping you'll let me have my job back."

Dylan held his breath. If Miss Bessie said no, Jennifer would have no reason to return to Casey's Cove. He wasn't ready to provide her with a reason himself, so he was counting on Miss Bessie.

"Some of the things I've told you weren't exactly the truth," Jennifer was saying. "I won't hold you to a final answer until you've had a chance to hear my story and make up your mind."

Dylan watched Jennifer's face, looking for a clue to what Miss Bessie was saying. Suddenly, Jennifer's green eyes filled with tears that overflowed and tracked down her cheeks.

His hopes fell. Miss Bessie had said no.

With the back of her hand, Jennifer wiped tears from her cheeks. "Thank you, Miss Bessie. I'll see you soon."

She hung up the phone.

"She agreed?" Dylan asked.

Jennifer nodded. "She said it didn't matter what I'd done, that I was to come straight home." She hiccuped as she tried to swallow a sob. "It's been a long time since I've had a place to call home."

Dylan felt like whooping with joy, but he kept a lid on his feelings. His heart and his head hadn't yet come to an agreement on what to do about Jennifer-Rachel.

"You'd better get packed," he said. "Miss Bessie's waiting."

Chapter Twelve

Dylan swung the last Christmas tree onto the trailer of the eighteen-wheeler and wiped sweat from his forehead with a bandanna. "You've had quite a crop this year, bro."

Jarrett signaled the driver, who started the heavily loaded rig down the mountain, then he waved Dylan toward the house. "I appreciate your help. Come on up. I have some cold brew in the fridge."

Dylan trudged up the steep incline toward the house where he'd grown up. Theirs had been a happy family, just the four of them, and Jarrett, five years older, had been both mentor and friend. He'd gladly stepped in to run the farm when failing health had necessitated their parents move to Florida for the warmer climate.

Dylan reached the house and settled in his father's rocking chair. The sinking sun beat on the worn boards of the porch, making the outside air comfortable, even in late November. Holding two frosty bottles by the necks, Jarrett stepped out of the screen door and let it slam behind him.

"Mom would get you for that if she was here," Dylan teased.

Jarrett handed him a beer and sank into a rocker next to him. "I wish she were here. I miss 'em both."

"Me, too."

Jarrett took a long pull from the bottle and stared out across the valley. "Lucky for you they're not."

"Why?"

"Mom would be all over you like a duck on a June bug for the way you're treating that girl of yours."

"I don't *have* a girl."

Jarrett fixed him with a stare that reminded Dylan of his father. "Others might believe that lie, but it won't wash with me."

"I never lie," Dylan protested hotly.

Jarrett shook his head. "I saw the way you looked at Jennifer when she first came here. And I know you took a chunk of your vacation days to travel to Atlanta to help her out."

Dylan shifted uneasily in his chair. "That doesn't make her my girl."

Jarrett ignored his protests. "And I've seen the way you've dragged around town the past month since coming back from Atlanta, looking like your dog died and somebody stole your truck."

Dylan squirmed again. Jarrett's comments were hitting too close to home. "I don't have a dog."

"Don't give me the runaround. This is your brother you're talking to. When was the last time you saw her?"

Dylan tried to ignore the loneliness and longing rising inside him. "About a week ago. At Raylene's."

"Did you talk to her?"

Dylan shrugged. "I said hello."

"Little bro, am I going to have to take you out to the barn and beat some sense into you?"

Dylan decided his best defense was to attack. "I don't see *you* settled down with a woman, and you're older than me."

"I have a good reason."

"Which is?"

"The right woman hasn't come along," Jarrett said without defensiveness.

Dylan snorted. "Are you expecting someone wearing a sign? How're you going to know the right woman?"

Jarrett took another swallow of beer and leaned back in his rocker. "That's easy enough. When I meet a woman I don't want to live without, I'll know she's the right one."

"Shoot, that's easy for you to say. It's a heck of a lot more complicated than that."

Jarrett smiled. "Why don't you tell me about it, then?"

Dylan plowed his fingers through his hair. "I don't want to live without Jennifer—"

"Aha," Jarrett snapped. "Didn't I tell you?"

"But I don't know if I can live with her, either," Dylan blurted.

"Why not?" Jarrett scratched his head. "She seems like an exceptionally fine woman."

"She is—in most ways."

"So what's the problem?"

Dylan breathed a sigh of regret. "I can't trust her."

"Whew, that's a pretty serious charge."

"She tells lies."

Jarrett rose from his chair, leaned against the porch railing and looked Dylan in the eye. "What kind of lies?"

Dylan downed the rest of his beer. "What does it matter? Lies are lies."

"Life isn't all black or white, bro."

"It is to me," Dylan insisted.

"Then you're going to grow into an unhappy, lonely old man," Jarrett said gently. "Are you miffed at Jennifer because of her false identity?"

Dylan nodded stiffly.

Jarrett crossed his arms over his chest. "Would you rather she'd remained Rachel O'Riley and that hit man had found her and killed her?"

"Of course not!"

"Then what should she have done?"

Dylan shoved to his feet, walked past Jarrett and gazed out across the valley where evening shadows deepened in the ravines. "She should have told *me*."

"That's funny," Jarrett said. "I thought you said she did tell you."

"She should have told me sooner."

Jarrett approached and slung an arm around his shoulders. "Maybe she wasn't sure she could trust you at first. After all, her life was at stake. Besides, you *are* the one she ultimately confided in."

''I can't stand lies. They can get people killed.''

Jarrett squeezed his shoulder. ''You're thinking of Johnny Whitaker, and in his case you're right. He and his mom might be alive today if he'd told you the truth. But Jennifer's case is different. Her lies kept her alive.''

''But—''

''No buts. Your moral compass makes you a fine man for the most part, Dylan. But don't let inflexibility rob you of what could be the love of your life.''

Feeling foolish, Dylan realized his brother was right. Jennifer's lies had harmed no one and had kept her alive, and she had ultimately trusted in him. More than anything else, however, he realized that he didn't want to live without her. The last month had been hell. He couldn't imagine the rest of his days without Jennifer in them.

Inside the farmhouse, a phone rang, and Jarrett went to answer it. He returned seconds later with a portable phone and handed it to Dylan. ''It's Raylene. She sounds pretty upset.''

Dylan grabbed the receiver. ''Raylene?''

''Thank God, Dylan.'' The waitress spoke so fast, she was stumbling over her words. ''I've been calling all over town to find you.''

''Slow down and tell me what's the matter.''

The waitress was practically sobbing. ''That hit man that was looking for Jennifer—''

''Michael Johnson?''

''I never knew his name. But he drove into town about ten minutes ago. He's in a different car, but I recognized him. I'm scared he's come for Jennifer.''

Fear flooded him. "Are you sure it's him?"

"Positive. I never forget a face, especially one as ugly as his."

"Have you warned Jennifer?"

"When I couldn't find you, I called the guest house and Miss Bessie's, but nobody answered at either place."

Horror gripped him at the possibility Johnson had already made a trip up Miss Bessie's mountain. "Which way was he headed, Raylene?"

"He wasn't headed anywhere when I saw him. Just sittin' in his car across from the Artisans' Hall."

"Keep trying Jennifer's number," he said. "I'm on my way there now. And call the PD and tell them what's happened. Have whoever's on duty meet me at the guest house."

"Trouble?" Jarrett asked when Dylan switched off the phone.

"The worst. That hit man's back in town."

Jarrett frowned. "If Jennifer's already given her testimony to the police, why would he still be after her?"

"I intend to find out."

Jarrett reached inside the screen door and grabbed his jacket and his hunting rifle. "I'm coming with you."

With Jarrett on his heels, Dylan raced to his truck, knowing as he ran that he was a good fifteen minutes or more behind Johnson.

A man with murder on his mind could do a lot of damage in fifteen minutes.

Praying that Jennifer wasn't home and that he and

Jarrett could intercept Johnson before the hit man reached her, Dylan put his truck into gear and burned rubber.

THE SUN had disappeared behind the crest of the western mountains, leaving the highway in deep shadows. Jennifer turned to wave at Sissy and her aunt, then pulled the car out of Millie's driveway. If she hurried, she'd be home before dark. Since her run-in with Crutchfield's hit man weeks before, crossing Bald Gap at night gave her the willies, and she was anxious to traverse the mountain crest before daylight disappeared.

She passed the turnoff to Jarrett's farm and thought instantly of Dylan. He was never far from her mind, even though she'd only seen him once since her return four weeks ago to Casey's Cove.

She'd been having breakfast at Raylene's last week. The doorbell had jingled, and there he'd stood, looking more handsome than ever in his dark green uniform. He'd ordered coffee to go at the counter, then turned and caught her eye.

"Hi." Her heart had pounded as if it would fight its way out of her chest.

"Hello," he answered with a guarded smile, as if he was afraid of revealing his emotions, and he looked uncomfortable at meeting her.

Grover brought his coffee then, and Dylan had paid and left without another word.

Raylene slipped into the booth across from her. "So how are things with you and Dylan?"

From anyone else, Jennifer would have resented

the question, but Raylene was a friend, and Jennifer needed someone to talk to. "Nowhere. That's the first time I've seen him since he brought me back from Atlanta."

"That's funny," the waitress said.

Heart aching, Jennifer frowned. "*Funny* isn't the word."

Raylene shook her head. "That's not what I meant. It's funny-odd he hasn't looked you up. Every time he comes in here, he asks about you."

Jennifer grimaced. "He's probably just checking to make sure I haven't broken any laws. He thinks I lack moral fiber."

"Pshaw," Raylene said. "Why would he think that?"

"All the lies I told." Jennifer shook her head sadly. "I didn't know what else to do at the time. Now I can't take them back. All I can do is say I'm sorry, but apologies obviously don't cut it with Dylan."

Raylene reached across the table and patted her hand. "I'm sorry, hon. That's the way Dylan is. Always has been, but his straight-laced attitude got worse after Johnny Whitaker was killed."

"Guess I don't have a chance, then." Jennifer sighed.

"Maybe it's just as well. Living with a man that unbending could be tough."

But he's not really like that, she had started to protest, then stopped. If he wasn't that obstinate, why hadn't he contacted her? Apparently he'd forgotten their lovemaking. She wished she could. Maybe she'd be less miserable.

Their encounter had been a week ago, and she hadn't seen him since.

The evening sky was deepening to a cobalt blue as she rounded Bottleneck Curve and entered the main street. When she passed the café, Raylene waved animatedly from the window, but Jennifer's thoughts were still on Dylan, and her response was a perfunctory flutter of her fingers as she passed by.

Torn by conflicting feelings, she started up the mountain toward the guest house. She had begun to think of Miss Bessie's place as home and of Miss Bessie as family. She hoped she could put down roots in the mountain valley where everyone had accepted her so warmly.

Everyone except Dylan.

He'd been remarkably proficient at avoiding her in the small town, and she wondered if she could be truly happy living in the same place, never seeing him, always hoping he'd appear. If she couldn't put her broken heart behind her, she'd have to move on. But she was·so tired of running. She longed to settle in one place.

Marry.

Have a family.

With Dylan.

Fat chance, she thought as she parked her car in the guest house drive. She might as well make plans to move on.

Lost in thought, head down, she trudged up the path toward the front porch. The telephone began to ring inside the house, and a dark figure stepped out of the bushes beside the steps.

"Dylan? Is that you? I won't let you scare me to death this time."

The man didn't answer.

Her eyes adjusted to the darkness, and she could barely make out the tough, ugly face of the man who confronted her.

One item she recognized instantly—the menacing silencer on the muzzle of the gun he aimed at her.

DYLAN JAMMED the accelerator to the floorboard and raced through town. Johnson's car no longer sat in front of the Artisans' Hall, and they hadn't passed it on the mountain road. The hit man had to be headed for Jennifer's place.

"Good thing you're a cop." Jarrett bounced in his seat and held onto his hat. "Or they'd put you under the jail for the way you zoomed through town."

Fearful his unlawful speed wasn't fast enough, Dylan prayed they'd reach Jennifer in time. The truck's engine whined from the strain of climbing up the road toward the guest house at such high speed.

Dear God, he prayed, *she can lie to me fifty ways to Sunday for the rest of her days. Just let her be all right.*

"Stop!" Jarrett yelled before they reached the guest house.

Dylan hit the brakes. "What?"

His brother grabbed a flashlight and shone it into the trees beside the road. The car Raylene had described was partially hidden by the underbrush.

Dylan yanked his gun from beneath the seat, hopped from the truck, and approached Johnson's vehicle.

"It's empty," he said to Jarrett when he returned to the truck. "He must have hiked on ahead."

"Should we follow in the truck?"

Dylan shook his head. "He'd hear us coming. We'll track him on foot. Make him think he has all the time in the world so he doesn't act too hastily. That may be our only chance to save her."

Using skills they'd learned in childhood, the brothers, obscured by the shadows, their progress inaudible, started up the road. When they reached the edge of the guest-house lawn, they remained hidden in the trees.

Dylan strained for signs of Michael Johnson, but the hit man was nowhere to be seen. Fortunately, Jennifer's car wasn't there either, which meant she wasn't inside the dark house. Dylan could hear the phone ringing, probably Raylene trying to reach Jennifer to warn her.

Suddenly an engine sounded behind them on the road. Jennifer's car was approaching. Searching for indications of a sniper, Dylan checked the darkened windows of the house.

No sign of Michael Johnson.

Miss Bessie's new Mercedes drove into view and pulled into the guest-house drive. Before Dylan could move, Jennifer had hopped from the car and started up the path.

He felt Jarrett stiffen beside him, and at the same

instant, saw Michael Johnson step out to bar Jennifer's way.

"Dylan?" she called. "Is that you? I won't let you scare me to death this time."

Johnson raised his gun.

Dylan tried to take aim, but Jennifer was in the way. He signaled to Jarrett who circled toward the left while Dylan moved to the right.

"What are *you* doing here?" Jennifer was saying, her voice amazingly calm for a woman staring down the muzzle of a gun.

Dylan's heart hammered in his chest. In a split second, Johnson could fire, his trained aim killing Jennifer before she fell. Dylan maneuvered for a clearer shot of the hit man.

"I have a contract to fulfill." Johnson's voice was cold, emotionless.

"But Crutchfield's in jail," Jennifer said, "and I've told my story to the police. What good will killing me now do?"

"Like I said," the raspy voice of the hit man floated across the lawn, "I have a contract to fulfill. I don't get my money until you're dead."

Dylan saw the hit man's finger move on the trigger. In desperation, he threw himself to the right and fired three shots.

Jennifer went down, and Johnson fell, too. The roar of gunshots echoed across the valley in the eerie night stillness.

The sound faded.

Nobody moved.

Guns at the ready, Dylan and Jarrett approached

the front walk. Jennifer lay in a heap on the bricks, her face hidden by her golden hair. Terrified of what he'd find, Dylan knelt beside her while Jarrett trained his rifle on the hit man.

Dylan reached for Jennifer's neck to check her pulse. His throat clogged with emotion, and he had to force out her name. "Jennifer?"

In a sudden move, she swatted his hand from her neck and sat upright. "You did it again! Scared me senseless! Why didn't you let me know it was you?"

He'd never been so happy to hear angry words in his life. "You're not hurt?"

"Not hurt?" She pushed her hair from her face and jammed her hands on her hips. "Just frightened out of my mind. I had no idea who you were and I thought you were shooting at me!"

Laughing with relief, he scooped her into his arms. "Thank God, Jennifer. I don't know what I'd do if he'd hurt you."

"This guy's wounded, but he's still alive." Jarrett still stood with the barrel of his rifle pointed at Johnson, who hadn't moved.

Flashing red lights and the sound of sirens broke through the trees, and a police car and rescue van roared up the drive. Within minutes, Gary Patterson, the paramedic, had Michael Johnson sprouting IVs and loaded on a stretcher while the cop took a statement from Jarrett.

Dylan stood with his arms around Jennifer. Whatever lies she'd told in the past seemed insignificant beside the fact that he'd come so close to losing her.

"How did you know Johnson was here?" Jennifer asked.

"Raylene saw him come into town. She warned me."

"And you came straight away?"

Dylan pulled her closer and nodded.

"Because that's your job?" Jennifer asked.

He shook his head. "Because I love you, and I'd die if anything happened to you."

"Honest?"

He drew back and gave her a stern stare. "You know I never lie."

She flung her arms around his neck and he kissed her as he'd wanted to for the last four weeks.

Epilogue

From the seat beside her on the plane, Dylan reached over and grasped her left hand, the one with the shiny new bright gold band that matched her engagement ring.

Jennifer—she'd grown fond of that name and decided to keep it—pulled her attention from the window and its view of North Dakota, spread out thousands of feet below them like a patchwork quilt in soft greens, golds and browns of early summer, streaked with the colors of the setting sun.

"Happy, Mrs. Blackburn?" he asked.

She squeezed his fingers and nodded. "Today has been the best day of my life."

He assumed a poker face, but his brown eyes twinkled. "I'm just glad I survived it."

"Survived?" she said in mock horror. "That's an awful thing to say about the day you're married."

"You know how us menfolk are about weddings. They give us the heebie-jeebies."

Her mock horror turned to outrage. "Dylan Blackburn—"

Before she could protest further, he leaned over and kissed her so thoroughly, her fury was forgotten.

"I admit," he said when she drew back for breath, "it was a great day. What part did you like best?"

"I couldn't begin to choose. The tears in your eyes when we pledged our vows—"

"Smoke caused that, from the candles." His eyes were twinkling again.

"Sissy McGinnis pelting everyone with rose petals from her flower basket."

Dylan smiled. "Even better was having her mother there watching, healthy and strong again."

Jennifer nodded. "And didn't Raylene look elegant in her bridesmaid's dress?"

He looped his arm over her shoulders and drew her close. "All I noticed about that dress was that it matched your eyes."

She snuggled happily in his embrace. "Dear Miss Bessie, she went all out for the reception. Three striped marquees on her front lawn, the string quartet—"

"And Tommy Bennett and the Mountaineers."

She smiled up at him. "I only stepped on your toes once during our wedding waltz."

"Maybe there's hope for you yet. I have to confess I've never seen a wedding cake quite like the one Grover made for us. Seven white layers and three of chocolate. The man's a genius."

She nodded. "Miss Bessie's freezing the top two layers for us for our first anniversary."

"That Miss Bessie is something else." He shook

his head in amazement, remembering. "I don't know how we can accept her wedding gift."

"The guest house? She'll be heartbroken if we turn it down. Besides, as long as we live there, we can help look after her." Jennifer glanced at her watch. "I suppose your folks are back in Florida by now."

"And we should be landing in Spokane soon."

"Spokane?" She sat upright. "I thought we were flying straight through to Vancouver."

Dylan grinned at her like a kid at Christmas. "Don't worry. We won't miss our Alaskan cruise. But I have some people I want you to meet first. I've rented a car to drive there."

"Dylan Blackburn, what are you up to?"

"There are some people I want you to meet," he repeated cryptically.

A few hours later, they had crossed the Montana state line in their rental car and turned off Highway 2 onto a secondary road.

"You know someone in Montana?" Dylan's secretive behavior had Jennifer thoroughly mystified.

"Not exactly."

He slowed the car, turned and drove beneath an arched sign with "Longhorn Ranch" burned into the wood in foot-high letters.

Jennifer bolted upright in surprise. "This is Wade Garrett's ranch."

Dylan nodded smugly. "Wade's expecting us. He's invited us to spend the night."

Their car traversed the long drive, and Jennifer caught her first glimpse of the century-old, two-story log house, just as Wade had described it in his letters to her.

"I wonder if he ever found the wife he wanted to raise his boy," she said.

Dylan pulled the car in front of the house and nodded toward the front porch. "Looks like he did."

Jennifer gazed at the people waiting on the steps, and her mouth dropped open in surprise. Wade Garrett, tall and lanky with a weathered tan and kind eyes, stood with one arm around his son, a thin child with the promise of his father's good looks. Wade's other arm was draped around a beautiful woman wearing a denim maternity jumper and a turtleneck red sweater.

Jennifer shrieked and grabbed Dylan's arm. "It's her. The *real* Jennifer! She's alive!"

"She calls herself Rachel now."

Dylan stopped the car and turned to her with a warm grin. "You *thought* she died, but she survived. She's alive and well—thanks to you. If you hadn't pulled her from that burning train—"

She slid down in her seat. "But how can I face her after stealing her identity?"

Dylan hugged her. "No problem. She thinks you did her a favor."

"By taking her name and identification?"

"By putting your name and Wade Garrett's in her backpack. When she gained consciousness, she had amnesia and thought she was Rachel O'Riley. The authorities contacted Wade from the note in her bag, and the rest, as they say, is history. Rachel and Wade were married last Christmas."

Jennifer smiled at him and said, "You're just full of surprises, aren't you?"

His eyes glowed warm with love and desire, and her heart filled with happiness. She placed her hand against his cheek, and he turned his head and pressed his lips to her palm.

"I promise," she said, "that I will never lie to you again."

"And I promise," he said in a voice husky with emotion, "that I will always trust you. Now let's greet the Garretts. They're anxious to meet you."

Jennifer left the car and raced toward the porch steps.

Rachel welcomed her with a hug, then pulled back and stared at her with eyes so like her own. "It looks like everything's worked out for the best, hasn't it?"

Jennifer glanced at Dylan, shaking hands with Wade and tousling Jordan's hair. Her heart swelled with love and contentment, and she linked arms with Rachel. "I couldn't agree more."

Together, the women who had exchanged identities to find happiness they'd never dreamed possible, followed their husbands into the house.

HARLEQUIN®
INTRIGUE

opens the case files on:

TOP SECRET
BABIES

Unwrap the mystery!

January 2001
#597 THE BODYGUARD'S BABY
Debra Webb

February 2001
#601 SAVING HIS SON
Rita Herron

March 2001
#605 THE HUNT FOR HAWKE'S DAUGHTER
Jean Barrett

April 2001
#609 UNDERCOVER BABY
Adrianne Lee

May 2001
#613 CONCEPTION COVER-UP
Karen Lawton Barrett

Follow the clues to your favorite retail outlet.

HARLEQUIN®
Makes any time special ™

HITSB

Harlequin truly does make any time special. . . . This year we are celebrating weddings in style!

A Walk Down the Aisle

WEDDING CELEBRATION

To help us celebrate, we want you to tell us how wearing the Harlequin wedding gown will make your wedding day special. As the grand prize, Harlequin will offer one lucky bride the chance to **"Walk Down the Aisle" in the Harlequin wedding gown!**

There's more...

For her honeymoon, she and her groom will spend five nights at the **Hyatt Regency Maui.** As part of this five-night honeymoon at the hotel renowned for its romantic attractions, the couple will enjoy a candlelit dinner for two in Swan Court, a sunset sail on the hotel's catamaran, and duet spa treatments.

Maui • Molokai • Lanai

To enter, please write, in, 250 words or less, how wearing the Harlequin wedding gown will make your wedding day special. The entry will be judged based on its emotionally compelling nature, its originality and creativity, and its sincerity. This contest is open to Canadian and U.S. residents only and to those who are 18 years of age and older. There is no purchase necessary to enter. Void where prohibited. See further contest rules attached. Please send your entry to:

Walk Down the Aisle Contest

In Canada	In U.S.A.
P.O. Box 637	P.O. Box 9076
Fort Erie, Ontario	3010 Walden Ave.
L2A 5X3	Buffalo, NY 14269-9076

You can also enter by visiting www.eHarlequin.com
Win the Harlequin wedding gown and the vacation of a lifetime!
The deadline for entries is October 1, 2001.

HARLEQUIN®
Makes any time special ®

PHWDACONT1

HARLEQUIN WALK DOWN THE AISLE TO MAUI CONTEST 1197
OFFICIAL RULES
NO PURCHASE NECESSARY TO ENTER

1. To enter, follow directions published in the offer to which you are responding. Contest begins April 2, 2001, and ends on October 1, 2001. Method of entry may vary. Mailed entries must be postmarked by October 1, 2001, and received by October 8, 2001.

2. Contest entry may be, at times, presented via the Internet, but will be restricted solely to residents of certain georgraphic areas that are disclosed on the Web site. To enter via the Internet, if permissible, access the Harlequin Web site (www.eHarlequin.com) and follow the directions displayed online. Online entries will be received by 11:59 p.m. E.S.T. on October 1, 2001.

   In lieu of submitting an entry online, enter by mail by hand-printing (or typing) on an 8½" x 11" plain piece of paper, your name, address (including zip code), Contest number/name and in 250 words or fewer, why winning a Harlequin wedding dre would make your wedding day special. Mail via first-class mail to: Harlequin Walk Down the Aisle Contest 1197, (in the U.S. P.O. Box 9076, 3010 Walden Avenue, Buffalo, NY 14269-9076, (in Canada) P.O. Box 637, Fort Erie, Ontario L2A 5X3, Cana

   Limit one entry per person, household address and e-mail address. Online and/or mailed entries received from persons residing in geographic areas in which Internet entry is not permissible will be disqualified.

3. Contests will be judged by a panel of members of the Harlequin editorial, marketing and public relations staff based on the following criteria:

   - Originality and Creativity—50%
   - Emotionally Compelling—25%
   - Sincerity—25%

   In the event of a tie, duplicate prizes will be awarded. Decisions of the judges are final.

4. All entries become the property of Torstar Corp. and will not be returned. No responsibility is assumed for lost, late, illegible incomplete, inaccurate, nondelivered or misdirected mail or misdirected e-mail, for technical, hardware or software failures c any kind, lost or unavailable network connections, or failed, incomplete, garbled or delayed computer transmission or any human error which may occur in the receipt or processing of the entries in this Contest.

5. Contest open only to residents of the U.S. (except Puerto Rico) and Canada, who are 18 years of age or older, and is void wherever prohibited by law; all applicable laws and regulations apply. Any litigation within the Provice of Quebec respecting the conduct or organization of a publicity contest may be submitted to the Régie des alcools, des courses et des jeux for a ruling. Any litigation respecting the awarding of a prize may be submitted to the Régie des alcools, des courses et des jeux c for the purpose of helping the parties reach a settlement. Employees and immediate family members of Torstar Corp. and D. L. Blair, Inc., their affiliates, subsidiaries and all other agencies, entities and persons connected with the use, marketing o conduct of this Contest are not eligible to enter. Taxes on prizes are the sole responsibility of winners. Acceptance of any pri: offered constitutes permission to use winner's name, photograph or other likeness for the purposes of advertising, trade and promotion on behalf of Torstar Corp., its affiliates and subsidiaries without further compensation to the winner, unless prohibited by law.

6. Winners will be determined no later than November 15, 2001, and will be notified by mail. Winners will be required to sign a return an Affidavit of Eligibility form within 15 days after winner notification. Noncompliance within that time period may resu in disqualification and an alternative winner may be selected. Winners of trip must execute a Release of Liability prior to ticke and must possess required travel documents (e.g. passport, photo ID) where applicable. Trip must be completed by Novembe 2002. No substitution of prize permitted by winner. Torstar Corp. and D. L. Blair, Inc., their parents, affiliates, and subsidiaries are not responsible for errors in printing or electronic presentation of Contest, entries and/or game pieces. In the event of printing or other errors which may result in unintended prize values or duplication of prizes, all affected game pieces or entrie shall be null and void. If for any reason the Internet portion of the Contest is not capable of running as planned, including infection by computer virus, bugs, tampering, unauthorized intervention, fraud, technical failures, or any other causes beyond the control of Torstar Corp. which corrupt or affect the administration, secrecy, fairness, integrity or proper conduct of the Contest, Torstar Corp. reserves the right, at its sole discretion, to disqualify any individual who tampers with the entry proces and to cancel, terminate, modify or suspend the Contest or the Internet portion thereof. In the event of a dispute regarding an online entry, the entry will be deemed submitted by the authorized holder of the e-mail account submitted at the time of entry Authorized account holder is defined as the natural person who is assigned to an e-mail address by an Internet access provic online service provider or other organization that is responsible for arranging e-mail address for the domain associated with submitted e-mail address. **Purchase or acceptance of a product offer does not improve your chances of winnin**

7. Prizes: (1) Grand Prize—A Harlequin wedding dress (approximate retail value: $3,500) and a 5-night/6-day honeymoon trip Maui, HI, including round-trip air transportation provided by Maui Visitors Bureau from Los Angeles International Airport (winner is responsible for transportation to and from Los Angeles International Airport) and a Harlequin Romance Package, including hotel accomodations (double occupancy) at the Hyatt Regency Maui Resort and Spa, dinner for (2) two at Swan Court, a sunset sail on Kiele V and a spa treatment for the winner (approximate retail value: $4,000); (5) Five runner-up prize of a $1000 gift certificate to selected retail outlets to be determined by Sponsor (retail value $1000 ea.). Prizes consist of on those items listed as part of the prize. Limit one prize per person. All prizes are valued in U.S. currency.

8. For a list of winners (available after December 17, 2001) send a self-addressed, stamped envelope to: Harlequin Walk Down Aisle Contest 1197 Winners, P.O. Box 4200 Blair, NE 68009-4200 or you may access the www.eHarlequin.com Web site through January 15, 2002.

Contest sponsored by Torstar Corp., P.O. Box 9042, Buffalo, NY 14269-9042, U.S.A.

PHWDACONT2

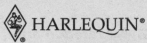

Where the bond of family, tradition and honor run as deep and are as vast as the great Lone Star state, that's...

Texas families are at the heart of the next Harlequin 12-book continuity series.

HARLEQUIN®
INTRIGUE

is proud to launch this brand-new series of books by some of your very favorite authors.

Look for

SOMEONE S BABY
by Dani Sinclair
On sale May 2001

SECRET BODYGUARD
by B.J. Daniels
On sale June 2001

UNCONDITIONAL SURRENDER
by Joanna Wayne
On sale July 2001

Available at your favorite retail outlet.

HARLEQUIN®
Makes any time special ®

Visit us at www.eHarlequin.com

HITT